CAPTIVE—OR DEATH

Shouts and gunshots came from every direction. Near the central fire ring, four white men, their ammunition exhausted, were held at bay by a band of hard-faced warriors.

"Don't kill them," Rebecca Caldwell called in Lakota. "We can get answers from them."

The white squaw stalked forward, her rifle slantwise across her body. "You men. Surrender and you won't be harmed. We want to know who sent you. Why did you attack the village?"

"You can go to hell, you half-breed!" one man snarled.

"That's not nice," Rebecca returned calmly. "Do you really want me to let these warriors have some sport with you? They won't kill you right away, of course, but you'll wish they had."

"Just like a damn half-breed. Crazy as a loon," the man snarled.

Methodically, Rebecca brought up her Winchester and shot Thern Miller through the calf. He howled with pain and fell to the ground.

"Now who set this up, mister."

"I'll tell you nothing," he replied.

Rebecca coolly shot off the toe of Miller's boot. "Just like mules," she stated flatly. "Some you can teach with kindness, others take force. I'll give you one more chance to answer my questions," the white squaw whispered as she cocked her rifle. "The next shot will be straight through your heart!"

#14

RED TOP TRAMP
—— BY E.J. HUNTER ——

ZEBRA BOOKS
KENSINGTON PUBLISHING CORP.

Special thanks to Mark K. Roberts for his assistance on this book.

ZEBRA BOOKS

are published by

Kensington Publishing Corp.
475 Park Avenue South
New York, NY 10016

First printing: May 1987

Printed in the United States of America

This episode of the adventures of Rebecca Caldwell is fondly dedicated to my Cherokee sister (GWY OV), Mary Ellen Edmunson, in hopes she enjoys it.

EJH

No woman since the Exodus has been subjected to such torment in her daily routine. Constantly moving from place to place, the object of shrill abuse, beatings, and the masculine prerogative, their lives were spent in toil and humiliation. Only death, usually in child-birth, brought surcease.

—William Flanders
Captive Women Among the Sioux

Chapter 1

To Lt. Arnulf Larsen, it could have been a scene played out in the anteroom of hell. A harsh, chill breeze rustled the brown, crisp-dry stalks of gamma grass and cut through even the thick blue wool of his tunic. High in the sickly-pale sky ice crystals twinkled like a myriad diamond pinpoints. It was not yet time for the damp, thick snows that mantled the Dakota prairie each winter, he thought thankfully. Off to the right, in the low skin lodge of the medicine man, a small drum throbbed softly. Arrayed behind him, a detachment of troopers suspiciously eyed a larger group of hard-faced Sioux warriors on the other side of the stone fire ring. The only warmth, and that scant, came from the council fire.

It certainly didn't emanate from Chief White Buffalo. Stooped with age, markedly bowlegged, with a round, protruding belly and stringy muscles in his limbs, Ptasan Okiye was civil chief of the Red Top Lodge band of the Oglala Sioux. His name, only two words in the Oglala tongue, had been shortened by the whites from White Buffalo Helps Him, for convenience. His seamed, weathered face had taken on a hostile expression and he glowered at the youthful cavalry officer.

A shiver of cold ran up Arnulf Larsen's spine and raised the fine black hairs on his neck. It's funny, he mused irrelevantly, people from the cold countries in Scandinavia thought of hell as being a place of terrible cold, being accustomed to it as a constant. Those from warmer lands, around the Mediterranean, had conceived of the place of eternal punishment as being blistering hot. After four years on the Great Plains, he tended to agree with the Norwegian version of hell. His pale blue eyes studied the determined Oglala chief opposite him.

Barely suppressed anger glittered in the obsidian chips of Ptasan Okiye's perpetually squinting eyes. Damaged though they were by years of participation in the Sun Dance as well as by the hereditary opthalmic defects of the Sioux, White Buffalo Helps Him's orbs did not lack in the ability to weigh men and determine their worth. He found the young pony-soldier chief truthful and sincere, if not in the least helpful.

The topic of their conversation centered on the invasion of Sioux treaty land by white cattlemen. So far they had met an impasse over a single element. The Oglala believed the treaty to be binding; the white men had changed the terms without a twinge of conscience.

"I have my orders, White Buffalo," Lt. Larsen stated again in his pleasantly thin tenor voice. "It is not I who made the rules. The Sioux are now required to live on the reservations. That includes the Red Top Lodge Oglala."

"What of the treaty that gave my people this land for so long as the grass grows and the sun should shine?" Ptasan Okiye protested through an interpreter.

"The times have changed. The old ways must give place to new ones," Larsen answered, hating the words he had to say.

"The Oglala want to live in peace, but the new white men do not honor the treaty and they kill the Oglala people."

Larsen shrugged. It had gotten back to the same point. "The same treaty of which you speak gave my people the right to travel freely across this land."

"Yes, but not to stay," came the quick reply. "You've let them come by numbers like the herds of buffalo. They kill the game, rip open our Mother, the Earth, and put up stakes and

8

metal rope that keep out our people. Now they come to our lodges at night and kill us. This isn't right. You know that, Lar-sen."

Through a sympathetic smile, which he tried to suppress, Arnie Larsen made a gruff reply. "It's wrong, and truly a crime, I think, that your people are being harmed. I'm sorry. I truly am, but there's nothing I can do unless you and your people live on the reservation. There are laws preventing white men from encroach . . . ah, taking lands from the reservation."

A tall, powerful man who stood beside White Buffalo Helps Him took a step forward. "Is not a treaty a law?" he asked in a growl.

"Ah, well, yes, it is."

"Then there was a law to keep the white men from staying in our country. That law is broken . . . by white men. Now you say there's another law. One that will keep the greedy ones from taking the reservation land. How long before *that one* is broken?"

The interpreter relayed this challenge, adding that the speaker was Blokanumpa, Two Bulls, a powerful war chief and head of the Brave Heart warrior society. Arnie Larsen's eyes shifted to a downward gaze. He sighed heavily.

"The truth in my heart makes me answer that there's no way of knowing," the young officer replied sadly. "It could happen at any time. Yet the fact remains that it is the law now. If you're on the reservation we can protect you. If you're not, then my chiefs call you renegade and hostile and you are hunted down with no mercy."

Two Bulls's lips curled in contempt. "It is as I expected." The next instant his words rang with anger. "If you can do nothing to help us, then we have to help ourselves."

Many of the assembled warriors muttered agreement. *"Hiye-hey-i-i, hiye-hey-i-i,"* while others called out encouragement, *"Hecito yelo! Hecito yelo!* That is true."

Ominously, the drum changed rhythm to that of the war dance. Several braves began the rapid, piston-legged, body-

9

twisting movements.

"Leave us, Lar-sen," Ptasan Okiye commanded. "There's nothing more we can say together."

Steel wheels clacked in staccato rhythm, lulling the passengers asleep in the warmth of midafternoon. The Fresno Line daily northern train rattled along the spur track that connected the Union Pacific with the Northern Pacific, north of the Black Hills of Dakota Territory. Rebecca Caldwell swayed gently with the rocking of the coach, and seated across from her, Brett Baylor—the man who called himself Lone Wolf—leaned back on the plush maroon velvet seat. Hat tipped forward onto the bridge of his nose, he snoozed lightly, a faint smile creasing his lips. The journey from Nevada had been a long one, and the frequently jerky motion of the train had not invited deep sleep. As though considering this, Rebecca spoke quietly.

"Not much further to go."

"Ummph! And then a whole day of blissful sleep, I hope," her companion responded in a sleepy voice.

"We could have taken a Pullman car," Rebecca suggested. "At least to the Frisco Line."

"What for? They still jolt these coaches hard enough to jar your teeth loose every time they stop or start."

"I swear you'd rather have come by horseback," Rebecca said with laughter.

"I'd rather have walked."

"It's nearly winter," she protested in mock innocence. "We'd never have made it this far."

Their conversation terminated the next instant when the steam whistle of the Baldwin No. 6 locomotive gave off a shrill hoot of five rapid blasts, the emergency signal. The big 4-6-0 locked its wheels and the steel began to shriek on the smooth track as the brakes took hold. Along the string of cars, brakemen swarmed to the big, horizontal iron wheels between cars and began to spin them rapidly to apply the added stopping power. Inside the coaches, many of the passengers came close to panic.

"What the hell!" Lone Wolf exploded.

In answer to his rhetorical exclamation, the conductor hurried along the aisle with oddly unsoothing words of comfort. "Nothing to worry yourselves over, folks. An emergency stop is all."

"I wonder what sort of emergency?" Rebecca questioned aloud.

Sparks flew from under the drivers as the heavy train, with its accumulated inertia of forty-five miles an hour, continued to slide down the rails. Eyes bugged, the engineer looked out the righthand window of the cab at the ripped-out track ahead, which grew rapidly closer. The speed had not yet diminished enough for him to throw the locomotive into reverse. With a sinking heart, he realized there would not be time.

"Jump, Louie!" he shouted to the fireman.

Then the two men hurled themselves from the cab a moment before the cow catcher glided beyond the disrupted rails. The pilot truck followed, driving the plow-shaped metal grille ahead of it into the track ballast as the four wheels dropped off the rail. The drivers came next, the ponderous weight of the boiler bearing down on them. The massive engine lurched and swayed, while gravel spewed out in a wide fan from the cow catcher. The momentum decreased slightly.

But not enough. Another tottering lurch, and the Baldwin slammed onto its side. A wide swatch of prairie grass and sod peeled outward as the forty-ton locomotive ground into the earth. Steam spouted from broken connections and popped safety valves. Still the internal pressures built from the disrupted equilibrium, until the boiler could contain itself no longer.

It exploded in a terrible roar of freed raw steam, abused air and disintegrating metal. The shock wave stripped planks off the passenger cars and sent several onto their sides.

11

"The horses!" Rebecca shouted as she held on desperately to the armrest while their car hurtled toward the brink.

"Look out for yourself," Lone Wolf yelled back over the pandemonium inside their coach.

Another grinding cacophany came from outside, then the surviving cars jolted to a stop. The lead truck of their own coach had slammed violently onto the churned-up roadbed, and the car slanted crazily off to one side. It teetered a moment, then came to rest.

Down the aisle a woman screamed hysterically. A man half rose from his seat, blood streaming from a cut on his bald head.

"Thank you, Jesus. Thank you, Jesus," he repeated over and over in an oddly distant voice.

"Help me!" a child shrieked. "Mommy, Daddy, where are you?"

"My leg," the conductor moaned. "My leg's broken."

Lone Wolf disentangled himself first and went to the railroader's side. Rebecca quickly followed. The former Crow warrior cut away the conductor's trouser leg, and Rebecca knelt to examine an unnatural bulge on the outside below his knee.

"You've broken it, all right," she said, tight-lipped, her face pale from the recent ordeal.

"There's other people, hurt an' scared. I've got to . . . got to . . . what'll I do?"

"Lay there and hurt while we see to them," Lone Wolf suggested tersely, though not cruelly.

"There'll be fire," Rebecca offered quietly.

"That's first, then," Lone Wolf acknowledged. "I'll find some other men who can get about and we'll go take care of it."

He left quickly, checking those in their car first. Rebecca gave the conductor a light, reassuring pat on the shoulder and started along the canted aisle. Dust, smoke, and steam obscured the view from the windows. Children cried frantically; some sobbed in terror, clutching at the bosoms of

12

unconscious mothers. The hysterical woman stopped abruptly to take on more air, then resumed an ululating wail that could have unnerved a corpse. Rebecca came to her and bent close.

"Stop that!" she shouted.

Louder than before, a howl of horror answered her.

"Listen . . . to . . . me! STOP THAT!"

Again no response, save another bellow of mindless fright.

Rebecca shook her head in momentary regret, hauled back her hand and slapped the woman soundly on both cheeks. "*Please!* Be quiet, dear. We're all hurt and afraid. That'll get you nothing."

"Wha . . . ? I-I-I . . ." Again a screech of hysteria erupted.

"I'm sorry," Rebecca declared.

She doubled her fist, took good aim, and punched the woman on the point of her chin. The pressure on the nerve center at the hinge of her jaw turned off her circuits. Her scream broke off in mid-howl. The disturbed matron uttered a soft grunt and slumped back on her tilted seat in trouble-free unconsciousness. Rebecca shrugged and looked at the astonished, mousey man next to her.

"I said I was sorry. There wasn't much else I could do."

"Oh, I wish I had done that," the woman's henpecked husband replied in a little bit of a voice, laden with wistfulness.

"She was upsetting the other passengers. You understand?"

He nodded, doffing his bowler hat. "*I'd* just like to have done it, for old time's sake," he replied with newborn self-confidence.

A young woman in the seat ahead had smashed her nose against the back of the seat in front of her. She bled profusely and had a glassy stare. Rebecca obtained a cold, damp cloth from the water jar at the front of the car and wiped away the carmine smear, then applied it to the girl's nose.

"Hold that and tilt your head back."

She moved on to help someone else. Wild whoops and shrill

13

cries drew her attention to the outside. A few shots crackled in irregular rhythm from the hillside. Then came a thunder of hoofbeats. Rebecca hurried to the window and looked out in time to see some twenty-five Sioux warriors charge down toward the derailed train, rifles firing, feathers flying, faces painted for war.

Chapter 2

A bouquet of arrows appeared, as if by magic, against the upslope side of the car, the impact of their points a ripple of sound. As the attackers drew nearer, Rebecca began to make out details of design and warpaint. To her astonishment, these warriors proclaimed by their beadwork and choice of color to be Šayaota, the Red Top Lodge band of the Oglala Sioux. It seemed she and Lone Wolf had returned to Dakota Territory in time for a full-fledged uprising. One with her own people right in the middle of it.

She had little time to ponder why or how this had happened. Glass began to shatter from the windows and the heartier among the passengers started to return fire. The women and children cried out in earnest now. Bullets spanged and howled off the heavy iron brake wheels and grab irons at the ends of the coaches. Hideously painted faces loomed closer with each passing second. Despite the knowledge that these were Iron Calf's people, Rebecca realized with a wrench that they didn't know she was aboard, and probably wouldn't care if they did. The lust for battle, she knew from experience, dimmed all of the finer sensibilities.

To them, on this train she was just another *wasicunwin*, a white woman. Spurred by this reflection, she hurried back to her seat and groped for her traveling bag. From it she extracted one of her heavy .44 Smith and Wesson American revolvers. She might hesitate at killing one of her Sioux relatives, she considered, but under these conditions, their horses became fair game. Rebecca knelt by a window as the Sioux split left and right to ride past the train. She brought up the .44 American and took aim.

Her first bullet missed. The second knocked a spotted pony out from under its rider. Squawling, it hit the dust and lay, kicking, for a moment before death overcame it. Damn. She hated killing animals. But the alternative pleased her less. Another shot. The last horse in the lefthand file reared and spilled its passenger before toppling to the ground. Now glass began to break on the opposite side of the car. Rebecca turned that way as the door burst open and three Oglala braves shoved into the aisle.

"Yuza!" Rebecca commanded in the Oglala tongue, then repeated, "Hold!"

Surprised to hear their language spoken among these hated whites, the warriors hesitated a second. Rebecca pressed her advantage.

"Hunkagapi, usi maya wo."

This further confused the young fighting men of the Red Top Lodge band. Who was this white woman who addressed them as previously made relatives and commanded their attention? Hesitantly, they advanced along the slanted aisle.

"Tuwe miwo he?" one of them asked.

"Šinaskawin, daughter of Iron Calf."

"Hiye, haya!" one doubtful brave exclaimed.

"Hiye-hey-i-i," muttered another. He knew indeed who she was. "If you are in truth Šinaskawin, why do you shoot at us?" he asked shrewdly.

"Because I like to live. You didn't know I was here. Why do you attack the iron horse?"

"Tokaha—it is the real enemy."

A large, fat brave pushed through the pair who had taken time to talk. *"Maka kin le,"* he shouted, *"mitawa ca."*

16

Rebecca produced a scornful expression. *"O'ko wayuwo!* Yes, you talk nonsense," she repeated. "You are spoiling for a fight, yet your words say you're still drumming up the courage to do so. You act like little boys."

The eldest of the trio nodded thoughtfully. "Šinaskawin is a warrior woman. Her words would be wise. Your words are wise. I am called Pasu Tanka," he added, rubbing the outsized proboscis that had inspired his name. "Come speak with our leader."

"Who is he?"

"Blokanumpa," came Big Nose's reply.

"Two Bulls. Yes, I know him well. He was still a child, playing with his *slukila* when I left your village on the Earthsmoke River," Rebecca responded in a tone of good humor, using the Oglala term for the Little White River.

"You've not been gone that long, Šinasakwin," Big Nose chided. "Two Bulls has twenty-four summers and two wives. He has no need to pleasure himself. Enough of this. Come, we will find Blokanumpa."

A lull came upon the battle as the three Oglala warriors and Rebecca Caldwell climbed from the train. Off toward the southeast, the small figures of running people could be seen, racing toward hoped-for safety across the waving prairie grass. Upslope slightly, on the opposite side of the wreckage, the Sioux braves sat their ponies, speculatively watching the damaged rolling stock. Big Nose led Rebecca in that direction.

"Who is she?" a young brakeman asked rhetorically.

"A friend of mine," Lone Wolf answered.

The youthful railroader frowned. He hadn't expected an answer. "What's she going up there for?"

"To try to save our hair from being lifted, I'd say," Lone Wolf suggested dryly.

Doubt colored the brakeman's words. "How can she do that? She's only a woman."

Lone Wolf formed an expression of disgust. He hated longwinded explanations. "Judgin' from the markings on these arrows, those warriors are from the Red Top Lodge band of the Oglala. That makes her not 'only' a woman, but the daughter of their former chief."

Face gone quickly pale, the teen-aged brakeman swallowed hard. "Oh, shit. You mean we've had *her* on this train all along?"

Lips twisted in loathing over such a racial slight, Lone Wolf made an uncommonly sharp reply. "She's white enough you'd never know. Whiter'n you, I'd judge, *boy.*"

Although sensitive about his station in life as a "high yellow," the young man refrained from reacting to the epithet. He'd heard and had to endure far worse from lesser men than this. He ran long fingers through his short, kinky orangish hair. So she was a mixed-blood. So what? He was, too. He chose, instead, to change the subject.

"Do, ah, do you think she can do anything? I mean, about keeping us from being massacred?"

"She can if anyone can."

Not satisfied with so simple an answer, the brakeman raised himself up to get a better look. Immediately a big .50 Sharps slug smacked into wood three inches about his head. He dropped down instantly, his face a sickly yellow-green.

"Ow, Lawdie!"

"Don't seem as if she's been too successful," Lone Wolf remarked lazily.

Ignoring the shot fired by a warrior nearby, Blokanumpa continued to stare hotly into Rebecca's level, deep blue eyes. From a distance, the tall, muscular war leader had not recognized her. Now, up close, he saw the woman he had watched grow from a girl into a wife and mother, married to his friend Four Horns. She had fought during the Crow raids and killed, as well. A true woman of the people, despite her fair

18

complexion and those startlingly sky-color eyes. Her heart-shaped face, with high cheekbones and a long, straight nose, sensual lips, and frequent smile could make any man's *ce* stiff as a war lance. How had she come to be on this iron horse?

"I ask Two Bulls again, why have the Red Top Lodge people attacked the iron horse?"

Not deigning to answer a woman directly, Blokanumpa formed his first words to the one called Šinaskawin.

"White Robe Woman, you are daughter of a man much honored in our hoop. We remember you. We mourned with you over the loss of Four Horns and your little son. We were cheered when you came to spend the last suns with your father, Iron Calf. With you, we mourned his going from us to the Great Spirit Land. It was a sign that he did so at the time of the battle with Yellow Hair on the Greasy Grass. You were there, too.

"But those times are past. There are new white men in our lands. The Army doesn't recognize the treaty anymore. They're saying we must be on the reservations or be counted as enemies. They protect those who attack us. Those who come with the stinking meat to graze away what food is left for the buffalo aren't punished. They are killing women and children among the Oglala and nothing is done to stop it. 'If you don't like it,'" Two Bulls said in a reasonable imitation of the soldier-chief, "'move onto the reservation. If you kill a white man, we will hunt you down and hang the lot of you.' We're not weak. We're not women. We remember how easily Custer fell."

"Yes, and at what price?" Rebecca countered. "They are using that as an excuse to punish you now. To let the white men take your land."

"She speaks the truth," a young, handsome Oglala put in. "I, Tatekohom'ni, have heard the words of the soldier-chief, Johansen. He says the same thing."

"Attacking women and children on that train won't do you any good," Rebecca urged. "It will only anger the whites more."

19

Two Bulls remained stubborn. "The council is angry. They have voted to have us carry the war pipe until the pony-soldiers see they are wrong and chase the white men out."

"But it's only some white men who are your enemy. Why not raid them, run off their cattle, instead of hurting these people who are innocent?"

"All whites are our enemy."

"That's not so! Think about it."

Two Bulls smiled. "I have been thinking. I saw that many of the white men threw down their weapons and ran like frightened children. Some even left their women and children behind. Others did not shoot at my brothers as we rode by. These are not the sort to attack our villages. Perhaps you're right. Often," he began on another track, "in the Grandfather times, when two warring tribes could not come to a simple way of ending the fighting, people of one tribe would go to live in the villages of the other, making an exchange. This way both sides would remain at peace, for fear of killing one of their own in an attack. It is a good thing. What I think . . . we'll take four hands count from among the children of these whites. They will come and live with the Red Top Lodge people, be one with us, until the white soldiers find a way to end the differences between us. You will come with us, to be a voice for our words."

"I, ah . . . I have a, ah, friend along. And spotted-rump horses from the Pierced Nose people. These things are mine and I value them."

"Then they will come with us."

"Still, the taking of hostages, all of this . . ."

"You doubt that we can do it?"

"Not in the least. Only . . ."

"Then it's done. Go and tell them of how the fighting will end."

"I'll go with her," Tatekohom'ni offered. His eyes held a glow of infatuation.

"Thank you, Whirlwinnd," Rebecca replied. "If one of you

is along, they may be more inclined to believe they are being spared."

Together, Rebecca and the handsome Sioux warrior returned to the train. Whirlwind showed her great honor by dismounting and walking at her side, rather than riding aloof as he would with an ordinary Oglala woman. The muzzles of many weapons bristled along the cars as they drew nearer. Lone Wolf crawled out from under the lead coach and came forward to meet them.

"We've got an end to the fighting," Rebecca explained quickly. "But there's a catch to it."

"Such as?"

"Blokanumpa, the *itancan,* wants hostages. Children from among the people on the train."

Lone Wolf scowled. "How's he think he can get away with that?"

"Simple. By offering everyone the chance to live by doing so. If not, he'll keep on attacking until everyone is killed."

"That's quite an offer."

Rebecca nodded. "One no one can afford to refuse. Two Bulls wants twenty children."

"My God. How do we break it to the people on board?"

"Good question, my friend. Should we have them draw lots? *Wakankan!*" Rebecca cursed. "That sounds so heartless. What other way is there?"

"What are you two saying?" Whirlwind inquired in Lakota.

"We are trying to decide how to tell the people about taking the children," Rebecca explained.

Whirlwind smiled broadly. "That's easy. Ask the children how many would like to come along and play at being wild Indians for a few suns."

"Crazy as it sounds," Lone Wolf remarked after hearing the translation, "I think he makes a lot of sense. Some of those kids, the boys especially, have shown a lot of grit. If they seem willing, their folks can hardly use that as an objection."

"Let's try it, then."

21

A quick count revealed only twenty-seven children aboard. Over loud protests and lamentations, fully fifteen of them clamored noisily to get to go along. When quiet had been restored, Rebecca appealed to her fellow passengers.

"I'm going along. I'm sure some of you women, particularly those whose husbands appear to have departed hastily, might be willing to go also. The children will have good care. That much I can guarantee. Once I have an opportunity to talk with the council, I'm sure that all of you will be released without harm. You could be safely in Pierre by, oh, a week from now."

"A-a week among those . . . those *savages*," one young mother wailed.

"Mrs. Archer, *I* spent *five years* living with these very people. This young man," Rebecca gestured to Whirlwind, "was a boy of eleven or so when my mother and I went to live in Iron Calf's village. I watched him grow. He *is not* a savage. None of them are. He's given his word, and so has the war leader, that the hostages will be turned over to the council, not abused or treated as captive slaves."

"What good's the word of a stinkin' Injun?" a portly drummer from the third passenger car asked in a surly tone. He swayed slightly and gave clear indication he had been partaking heavily of the bottle he clutched in his left hand.

"In this instance, it's better than what they offered if we refuse."

The inebriate blinked his eyes at Rebecca and wet thick lips. "An' whassat?"

"We trust them, go with them to the encampment, or they'll stay here and keep attacking the train until they kill us all," Rebecca told him heatedly.

"Including you?" the high yellow brakeman demanded owlishly.

"Oh, they might try to spare me, but bullets don't have eyes and neither do arrows. There's small chance I'd survive."

"Yer damn' tootin', missy," the drummer snarled. "We'd see to that. Ya can't trust a half-breed any more'n you can a fullblood. Most likely she's plottin' with 'em to get us all

22

butchered, I say."

"And *I* say you'd better watch that mouth of yours, or I'll knock it around on the other side of your head," Lone Wolf injected in a pleasant, conversational tone.

Whirlwind laughed sharply, then pointed rudely at the fat, drunken salesman. He rattled off a liquid sentence in Lakota.

"Whirlwind just said that if the Oglala shot you, you wouldn't bleed, you'd only squirt out whiskey." Rebecca supplied the translation.

"Yer greasy frien' tryin' to say I'm . . . I'm . . . ulperah, drunk?"

"No one could have put it more eloquently than you, sir," Rebecca told him sweetly. "Now, since you have no children, and hence no vested interest in this debate, I'd suggest you keep your goddamned mouth shut or I'll gleefully save the war party the effort of shooting you."

For a moment the drummer's mouth gaped. He managed to start it working, but it moved in silence a second before any sound came. "You wouldn't kill a white man."

"I'm a *half-breed*, remember?" Rebecca told him icily. "I can't be trusted. As I recall, you made that astute observation yourself, not two minutes ago."

"Mom," a clear, youthful voice piped up. "Please, Mom, I want to go."

"Hush, now, Tommy. You're only eleven. Boys your age know nothing of what's good for them."

"You think dying before he reaches twelve is better, madam?" Rebecca inquired.

Clarissa Archer, Tommy's mother, paled and blinked her eyes rapidly. She wrapped protective arms around her child. Tommy wriggled and squirmed to break free.

"This—this is . . . *inhuman*," his mother blurted.

Suddenly the slender, towheaded youngster underwent a dramatic change. He swelled his chest and yanked himself free of his mother's enveloping grasp. Eyes flashing, he turned on her.

"Daddy ran away like a yellow cur dog. Now you want me to

23

stay here and get us all killed. *That's* 'inhuman' to me. Lemme go."

"Yeah! Me, too!" another boy yelled.

"An' me. Lemme go with them."

"Me, too! Me, too," a girl of nine or so demanded.

Tommy slipped the suspenders from his shoulders and literally ripped his shirt off. He started to remove his trousers also, but Whirlwind reached out and stopped him. The boy scowled at the Sioux brave as Whirlwind uttered a few chopped syllables in Lakota.

"He says, 'Later. Then we'll get you a loincloth and some moccasins,'" Rebecca informed the boy.

"Oh, boy! That's swell!" Tommy enthused.

"Hiyupo! Hiyupo!" Whirlwind commanded, waving his arm in a gesture to draw the children forward.

Tommy's mother began to weep, as did several other women. Defiantly, the fifteen volunteers managed to evade their parents and form together in a group at Whirlwind's side. Reluctantly, a boy of eight shuffled his feet as he, too, broke away and joined the others. When no more came forward, Whirlwind pointed out four more and indicated they should come away from their mothers' sides.

"We'll report this," Tommy's mother threatened. "Don't you think for a moment we won't. You're in a lot of trouble, young lady."

"That may well be. Only, I'd think about one thing. This way at least you're alive to make that report."

Whirlwind drew Tommy close to him and ruffled the boy's hair. "Mahtociqala," he said affectionately. "Mahtociqala." Then, to the others, *"Hakamya upo."*

As though understanding his command to come, to follow him closely, the children marched off in good order behind the tall Oglala. It's good, Rebecca thought warmly. Within a day, little Tommy Archer would be Small Bear to everyone in the war party. And a bloody slaughter has been avoided, by a small boy's courage, she concluded gratefully.

24

Chapter 3

Over the high, bristly, brown expanse of a prize seed bull's back, Grover Ridgeway gazed steadily into the florid face of his visitor. Ridgeway's lean one-hundred-sixty-pound frame remained at rest, though the twin crescents of white at the corners of his mouth would have revealed to a more sensitive observer the degree of his unease. Alystaire Carmoody lacked that requisite perception.

Long before his present fifty years, unkind wags at school had tagged Alystaire Carmoody with the unlovely sobriquet of "Piggy". Balding, with a fringe of salt-and-pepper hair, his eyes deep-set in fat cheeks, Carmoody's present appearance did little to dispel that porcine comparison. His short-fuse temper, which kept his face perpetually flushed, along with pursed lips and a nose smashed by a rebellious cowhand, added color to his snoutlike visage.

The information he had just conveyed to Ridgeway caused the latter's discomfort. "Carter an' some of the boys hit the Sioux again last night," Carmoody had said. Now he waited for some reply, expecting approbation.

"Aren't those gunhawks of yours moving a little fast?"

Carmoody's fleshy jowls quivered in reaction to the nature of the question. "All of us are in agreement on this, Grover. You as much as the rest. As I recall it, you called the Indians, ah, 'wild animals like the buffalo and prairie dogs, only a bit more dangerous.' Wasn't that it?"

Ridgeway frowned. "Yes, but by 'removal' I had in mind leaving them alive, once we pushed them off that prime grazing land."

A scowl turned down the corners of Carmoody's mouth and developed deep furrows on his excessive expanse of forehead. "What was it Napoleon Bonaparte said about breaking eggs to make an omelet? If these Sioux vermin resist, the boys can't simply let themselves be killed. Look, someone is going to have that land eventually. I intend for it to be the seven largest ranches in Dakota. These stray bands of Oglala and Mineconjou are a menace to commerce and an obstruction to progress. They have to be put on the reservations. The government says so, the Army's trying—though I think not hard enough—and I'm damned determined to see it done. Why, once they're out of the way, we can end up owning pretty near all of the territory."

"The miners up Deadwood way might not agree with that." Ridgeway pulled a wry expression.

"To hell with that. Those sourdoughs only want to pick and pry in the rocks for gold. They don't give a damn about all that grass going to waste on buffalo and Indian ponies"

"But we do."

"Yes, damnit, *we do!*"

Face the color of a Duroc boar in rut, Carmoody emphasized his point by a slap on the broad withers of the bull. The powerful beast gave a liquidy snort that showered droplets of saliva on both men, and then it stomped an impatient hoof. Ridgeway reached over and scratched the bovine mountain behind one ear, soothing it.

"So what is it you expect from me now?" Ridgeway queried.

"We need some more men if we're to go after that little village to the north. Say, twenty of your hands to join with the rest. You've got the biggest spread, next to mine, so it's only fair you contribute more men than someone like, say, Branch Delano."

"I can't spare twenty hands. We're busy rounding up the herd to drive to winter pasture."

"How many, then?" Carmoody was determined to get what he wanted.

Grover Ridgeway considered the matter a moment, lips screwed into an askew pucker. "Oh . . . six, eight, maybe."

"Less than a dozen men! Damnit, with the Association range detectives I've got on my payroll, I have forty-three men committed to this. The least you could do is give up fifteen."

"Alystaire, I've only *got* twenty-one men, counting my sons, Dave and Gordon."

"Bull crap."

"I only fill up the bunkhouse for the spring roundup and branding, and for the drive to the railhead. This is a hell of a poor time of year to be pulling men off their jobs for something like this."

"Mark my words," Carmoody said darkly, "if we don't finish this now, by next spring, someone else will have all that prairie fenced off and turned to the plow. You don't want a bunch of damned clodhoppers for neighbors, do you?"

Ridgeway's expression changed and he spoke reluctantly. "No. You've a point there. This is prime cattle country. No room for damned farmers. All right, but only twelve. I can't lose what stock I've got to a blue norther in order to acquire land I wouldn't need then, for want of cattle to graze on it."

"Good. Day after tomorrow, have 'em at my place. We're gonna stir up enough conniption among the Sioux that we can sit back and let the Army do our killin' for us."

Frost had used a broad paintbrush on the scattered cottonwood and beech trees. Bright yellow, orange and gold outnumbered the surviving pale green leaves. The sky, a deep, bottomless blue, stretched to each horizon without a hint of cloud. Even a month earlier it would have been uncomfortably hot. Now a chill breeze moderated the temperature and made

27

travel easy. Rebecca Caldwell rode at ease on her Appaloosa stallion, Sila. He had a thick plaster over some scrapes on his chest, acquired when the stock car derailed. At that, Rebecca considered him lucky.

One of their precious animals had broken a leg and had had to be destroyed. Fortunately, it had been one of two geldings. The others had received varying degrees of injury. The Oglala had provided ponies for the hostage women and children from their reserve mounts. The little caravan moved steadily across the Dakota prairie at a fast pace. Lone Wolf rode ahead, sign-talking with one of the Oglala warriors. Rebecca found herself hock-to-hock with the youthful Tatekohom'ni. Whirlwind flashed her a warm smile and spoke in Lakota.

"I remember you. You fought like a panther when the Crow attacked our village."

"I lost my husband and son," Rebecca reminded him.

"Yes, and lay sick for a long time. I . . . " Scarlet colored Whirlwind's face. "I cried for you. To grieve your loss when you were with the Spirits and could not yourself. See this?" He extended his left arm and revealed a long white cicatrix of a knife slash. "I cut my hair and my arm for you. I think— though I was a boy of but fourteen summers—I think I was in love with you."

Touched by this revelation, Rebecca warmed toward the Oglala brave. They talked on for a while of mutual acquaintances and close friends. Last, he spoke of Iron Calf's death from old age at the Greasy Grass, now nearly two years in the past.

"I wanted to speak to you then. To claim you for my own," Whirlwind stumbled out. "But it was not the time. Not with your grief."

Rebecca felt herself stirred by this ardent admission. "My, but you're bold. Sioux boys usually play the flute to declare themselves to their beloved."

Whirlwind made a gesture of embarrassment and impatience. "I shouldn't have spoken like that. Is bad manners.

28

That man you are with . . . he is your husband?"

"Lone Wolf? No. He helped me get away during that last battle with the Crow. He was a Crow warrior, but he is no longer."

"He was a white man once, but he is no longer," Whirlwind replied astutely.

"You see things very clearly for one so young," Rebecca complimented him.

"I'm not so young as you would think," he shot back. "No, Sinaskawin, I don't mean it that way."

She reached out, boldly so for Oglala custom, and touched him lightly on the arm. "I do. I, ah, find myself unable to stop looking at you. I hear flute music, even when none is playing. At night, my sleeping robes are cold and unpleasantly empty. I find myself wanting someone to fill them with me."

Whirlwind discovered his attitude toward this risqué talk in the form of a thundering erection. Many were the nights, as a timid youth, that he had fantasized the presence of her beautiful body beside him in his sleeping place. Now, why now she practically offered herself to him. He couldn't believe his good fortune. Could she really mean it?

Her tender smile answered him, before her full, sweet lips parted to speak. "If you came a-courting, I'd not turn my blanket away, Tatekohom'ni."

Whirlwind thought he would burst. Although only technically still a virgin—the sum-total of his experience being limited to shy mutual exploration under the blanket with the two girls he had courted so far—he had never had a lush, full-blown woman open her blanket to him like this. The sensation nearly had him undone. One more sliding touch of his loincloth across the sensitive tip of his penis and he would be embarrassed to the point of humiliation. With the most soulful groan of his entire eighteen summers, Whirlwind yanked on the braided-hair jaw rein of his pony and drummed his heels into its ribs. At a distance of fifty jumping paces, he let out a wild yell of delight, then searched for a stream to wash away the stain of his incontinence.

"I detect a boy who has found himself a man lost to love," Lone Wolf remarked as he reined back to Rebecca's side.

Rebecca's eyes twinkled merrily, although she said not a word.

Two of the smaller children began to cry shortly before sundown. All signs of white civilization had disappeared the previous day. The realization of being surrounded by painted warriors and completely at their mercy had finally taken their toll. Rebecca trotted Šila back to where a harried young woman from the train tried to console the wailing pair.

"There now, there," the white squaw soothed. "There's nothing to be afraid of. We're going to stop soon for the night. Then we'll have some nice, juicy antelope steaks."

"Aaaawwoo," a red-headed moppet howled. "Don't like an'elope. It tastes like goats smell."

"Quit bein' such a sissy, Stevie," Tommy Archer growled at him as the lad rode up.

True to the promise made at the train, Tommy had been outfitted with spare clothing from Whirlwind's war bag. He wore nothing but a breechcloth and an oversized pair of moccasins. A beaded headband kept his mop of unruly yellow hair out of his eyes, and Rebecca suspected he still pouted about not being given an eagle feather to wear in it. He sat his Oglala pony bareback, and the sun, rather than turning him scarlet as Rebecca had anticipated, had already begun to brown his considerable expanse of exposed skin.

"A-aren't you sc-scared, Tommy?" Steve blubbered.

"*'Scared?'*" Tommy taunted him. "What's there to be scared about?"

"Don't you miss your folks?"

Tommy rubbed one palm against his bare chest. "Nope. I love it out here. I'm really free."

"No, we're not," Stevie managed, his voice rising to a wail.

30

"We're . . . we're prisoners!"

"Bull you-know-what," Tommy said through a sneer. "We get to swim, and fish, and hunt, and ride horses. I don't call that bein' a prisoner. I'm never goin' back. I wanna live with Blokanumpa forever. He says I'm not too old to learn to be a warrior. No more tight clothes, no more school, no more, ugh!, *church*."

"*Tommy Archer*," young Miss Hawthorne, a schoolteacher screeched. "You're worse than these savages. You've frightened these children quite enough, besides. You ride that horse like a wild man. And the way you're dressed is shameful. Why, you're nearly naked."

"I could be all naked if I wanted to an' Blokanumpa wouldn't pester me about it," Tommy returned defiantly.

Sally Hawthorne's eyes narrowed. "I've a mind to turn you over my knee and switch you right proper."

"You do an' Two Bulls'll lift yer hair. No more slateboards, no more books, no more teachers' dirty looks," Tommy chanted in a singsong soprano as he kicked his pony's ribs and rode off. "I only wanted to help," he threw back over his shoulder.

"I think he did want to help us," Rebecca put in before Sally could vent her outrage. "He's a young boy on the verge of adolescence."

Sally Hawthorne sniffed indignantly. "You've lived with these very savages who have stolen us away. You can hardly expect to be treated like decent folk."

"*I*, too, thought I could be of some help with the frightened ones. Like Tommy, I was apparently mistaken," Rebecca told her coldly. "I think I'll go ride with Tommy a while. I find I prefer his company a hell of a lot more than yours, sister."

Gape-mouthed, Sally Hawthorne was left alone with the unsettled children. She watched through angry eyes as Rebecca Caldwell rode to where Tommy Archer had taken his place in the file next to the warrior called Whirlwind. *That* one had assumed entirely too much liberty with the shameful white

31

squaw. But then, Sally considered, like seeks like, even among savage trash. She growled in righteous indignation when she saw Rebecca reach over and impulsively hug Tommy.

Supper had ended shortly before the sun set and the fire was put out. The antelope had been enjoyed by everyone but Sally Hawthorne and Steve Fuller. There had been little conversation, the one group being unable to communicate with the other. Although, to Sally's disgust, Rebecca had kept up a regular discourse with several of their captors in their heathenish tongue. Tommy Archer had acquired enough words to make an occasional comment. Some of them had elicited bursts of grunting laughter from the warriors, and they looked speculatively at Sally.

For the first time since the assurance of not being harmed had been given, Sally began to fear a fate worse than death. It would be just like them. All that grunting and moaning, the slap of one bare body against another, the immense pressure and that sudden burst of pain, the dirty feeling of something long, hard and decidedly male sliding . . . with a shiver of what she tried furiously to assign to fear, Sally tightened the blanket around her and went to sleep.

Rebecca Caldwell and Whirlwind did not sleep, no matter the quiet of the camp. They lay restlessly in their sleeping robes until certain that slumber had come to everyone else. Then they gathered their things and stole off to the shelter of a low willow beside the creek, downhill from their camp.

They made a soft, comfortable palate with the blankets and buffalo robes. Then Rebecca removed Whirlwind's hunting shirt. Next she took off his loincloth. Rebecca touched him lightly.

"Ummmm," she murmured. "That's a *sluka* a man can be proud of."

"I am," he answered in a teasing tone. "I have been ever since I was a little boy."

Rebecca looked at him hungrily. She had changed from her white woman's traveling clothes the previous afternoon before they left the wrecked train. Now she dipped slightly to take the hem of her elkhide Oglala dress and pull it upward. Her soft, half-length underskirt of pounded buckskin rustled softly as she removed her outer garment.

"We didn't come here to talk," she whispered breathlessly. "I have a great deal more interest in feeling what Man Maker gave you." As she spoke, Rebecca untied the thong at her waist and removed her *nitohompi.*

Moonlight made her bare breasts glow as they stood rigidly out from her chest. Her lithe form seemed almost to be that of a water nymph, and filled with boyish visions, Whirlwind eyed her avidly, aching inside, while his heart pounded and blood roared through his veins. She was all he had imagined and much more. It took all of his will to keep from spilling his life force the moment she reached over and circled his flesh with warm, soft fingers. Slowly she sank to her knees before him.

"*A-i-i-i!*" he keened as she flicked her tongue to his heated flesh. "*Ho, ho, waśte. Ceazin waśteśte.*"

Yes, yes, good, Rebecca thought the words in English. "Yes, it's very good," she said aloud in Lakota.

Whirlwind began to writhe and to thrust his hips back and forth. Rebecca loved it every bit as much as he. His rapid response and fragile nearness to his peak excited her. Gladly she accepted the challenge to give her all, yet keep him from exploding far too soon.

Whirlwind shivered and trembled. Starbursts went off inside him. Rebecca sensed her own passions growing. She continued her lovemaking more ardently, creating new surges of joy for both of them. Whirlwind became more restive, then frantic, then unhinged, as his time came to fulfillment.

He burst forth in a shower unlike anything since his childish promise to stop self-pleasure, which he saw as unwarriorlike. His vow had endured for a long, tormented week. His reward had been a thorough shower of sap quite as powerful and plentiful as what Śinaskawin had brought forth. Transported, he bit at his lower lip to keep from howling at the moon like a crazed coyote.

When the last wild sensation became memory, Rebecca drew Whirlwind to her and they lay on the pile of robes. Her curious fingers explored his body, while he searched out the secrets of hers.

With consummate skill, she kept him from impaling her all at once, admitting only a bit at a time. "I want more," he groaned. "Please."

"You'll get it," she promised. "The greatest sweetness of love is the ache that comes from prolonging it. But, oh, oh, yes, I feel it now. It's going to be so won-der-ful. . . ." Rebecca managed before she released her grip and allowed her powerful young eighteen-year-old lover to drive himself in to the hilt.

She wanted to shriek with delight. Her head swam as he began a plunging, irregular rhythm that drove his ample maleness deep within her. Her hips began to piston, driving to enforce a mutually satisfying tempo. Whirlwind caught on to it and responded, matching his stroke to her thrust. Whirlwind's mouth covered one of Rebecca's hard-nippled breasts. His loins radiated unbearable heat and the tingling waves of sheer marvel that washed over him seemed to sap away all his energy. Yet, onward they struggled. Rebecca shook with the intensity of her pleasure.

"*Waśte,*" she gasped. "*Hiye-hey-i-i, waśteśte, waśteśte!*" She wailed at last as she sped upward to the pinnacle and tumbled off for the first time. "Keep going!" she panted immediately. "Don't stop, don't ever stop!" she pleaded. "Tatekohom'ni, you . . . are . . . a . . . miracle!"

Like a star gone nova they swelled slowly and brightly until they burst into oblivion together. Their miraculous bonding continued while the moon set and the stars wheeled to the far side of the sky.

Chapter 4

White puffs dotted the sky the next morning, like patches of powder smoke from distant artillery. Lt. Col. Bryce Peyton took the morning formation at Camp Cullen, as was his usual practice. At five-foot-six, he had to look up to exchange salutes with his adjutant, who had just reported the three companies of cavalry all present and accounted for, named the troop designations of the three companies absent on other duties, and reported those on hand ready to hear the Orders of the Day.

"Very well," Colonel Peyton replied in a buzzsaw tenor. "Mr. Adjutant, post the orders of the day."

Tall, lanky Major Varney saluted once again. "Sir, yes sir!" He executed a crisp about-face, raised a sheet of paper at arm's length and bellowed out loudly enough for all to hear.

"Attention to orders. Published this third November, eighteen seventy and eight. Company A to stable duty and tending of harness until noon mess formation. Company C to wood and water detail all day. Draw rations from the mess hall. Company E mounted drill until noon mess formation. Afternoon, Company A and Company E to cut brush and burn grass to a distance of three hundred yards from the stockade. Headquarters Company, to maintenance of records and correspondence all day. Also cleaning of headquarters building. Gardeners are excused from fatigue duty. There will be a company sing fest following retreat formation and evening mess. Sergeant major, dismiss the companies."

"Sir, yes sir!" the burly three-striper rang out. After the ritual salute and about-face, he threw back his head and bellowed. "Companies . . . dis—miss!"

The usual controlled and quiet pandemonium followed as the unmounted troopers hurried to remove their unneeded shell jackets and make ready for breakfast. Colonel Peyton and Major Varney went inside the headquarters building and down a hall to the officers' mess. There the junior officers already inside stood to rigid attention while their superiors went leisurely to the chow line and accepted plates laden with buffalo gravy on biscuits, eggs, and oatmeal. To this they added thick, handleless cups of steaming coffee. Crossed cavalry sabers had been painted on the sides of the cups, against a background shield of yellow. Peyton and Varney seated themselves, and normalcy returned to the room.

"Goddamnit, Ed," Peyton began as he drove the side of his fork tines through a biscuit. "I don't like this one bit. Something, or someone, is stirring up the Sioux, yet those deskbound featherheads in Washington won't let us do anything about it."

"Unless there's a proven hostile act by the Indians," Ed Varney amended while he munched on the thick cream gravy studded with tiny chunks of buffalo meat.

"Something we'll have hell's own time proving," Peyton groused.

The short, energetic lieutenant colonel speared the yolk of an egg and muddled its runny yellow material into the edge of his buffalo SOS before scooping up a forkful of the result. He chewed with the same precise, rapid motions he applied to all his activities. White bits of his breakfast clung like hoarfrost to the strands of his full, drooping mustache.

"Goddamnit," he went on. "Custer had the right idea. Kill 'em all and let God sort 'em out. Only those idiot civilians back

36

East have gone soft on the savages. Here we are, surrounded by hostiles, outnumbered four or five to one and we can't even thin the opposition ranks a little without justifiable cause. It's enough to make a grown man cry, Ed."

"I haven't noticed any tears on your cheeks, Bryce," Varney responded dryly.

"I save 'em for when I'm home with Elizabeth."

"Ah, Elizabeth. A strong woman, steadfast and brave. A darned good cook, too. You're fortunate to have her along with you. Which reminds me. Are you and the lovely Mrs. Peyton going to grace the songfest this evening?"

Peyton made a sour face. "I don't suppose there's a graceful way of getting out of it. I know that somewhere among the troopers are some men with beautiful singing voices. Although for some reason known to God alone, they never seem to volunteer for these vocal contests of yours. I'm afraid that this evening all we'll get is the usual collection of laryngitized crows."

"You're hypercritical, Bryce," Varney riposted through a chuckle.

"I'm prejudiced. I *know* what we'll get. Sergeant O'Marah singing "The Rose of Trahleigh," a guttural, incomprehensible rendition of "Die Loralei" by Corporal Gutterman and Private Junker, and of course our very own Privates Tanner, Thurmond, and Tydewell with a tearfully cornpone rendition of "Lorena." But I'll be there, all the same. Honor of the regiment and all that."

Colonel Peyton had completed his breakfast and returned to his office, the sun had climbed to a steep angle of nine o'clock, and the yardbirds from the guardhouse had swept clean the parade ground of horse dung, when a yelling civilian atop a lathered horse raced rapidly toward Camp Cullen. The news he brought galvanized the colonel into instant action.

"Sergeant major, have Company A's trumpter sound "Boots and Saddles." Now what was this again?" he demanded of the gasping, pale-faced man.

37

"Injuns. The damn' Oglalas, they done attacked the train."

"*Which* train, man? And go slow."

"The *Frisco Flyer* from Omaha to Billings. They pulled up rails, wrecked the locomotive and several cars, captured some women and children, and hauled them away to God knows where. Happened three days ago."

"How is it that I'm only now learning about it?"

"Dunno. I had me some fellers from the train come by my place, wanted to borrow some horses. I didn't give 'em none, but I hightailed it right over here, Colonel. I know how you feel about the redskins."

A cold smile of satisfaction quirked up the corners of Peyton's mouth. "Ah . . . yes. Enough said about that. How many were killed?"

"Three, least that's what these fellers said. Coulda been more."

"You're sure it was the Oglala?"

"They brung by an arrow. I judged it by its markings to be Oglala. Red Top Lodge band, at that."

A wild, wavering beam lighted Peyton's eyes. He seemed to be looking far off into the distance. "White Buffalo, at long last I'm going to hang some of your cantankerous braves. Sergeant Major, send in Lieutenant Larsen the moment he gets here."

"Yes, sir."

"Can you tell me anything else?"

"No, Colonel. Only that a large party of Sioux, with the captives, headed northeast from the wrecked train."

"That'll do for now, then. Yes, that'll do quite well. Larsen's a damned Injun-lover. Let's let him get a close look at what these hostiles have done and then see how nice he thinks they are."

"Miss Rebecca, is it far to the Indians' village?" nine-year-old Rachel Tilton lisped. Her big blue eyes looked up anxiously at the white squaw.

38

"No, Rachel, it can't be much further. They tend to camp along a regular route. The country here is familiar to me. Over that rise should be a big, round valley, like a soup plate."

"Did you really live with these Indians?"

"Yes. For five years."

"How old were you?"

"Fourteen when my mother and I went to Iron Calf's village."

"It must have been awful."

Rebecca's brow wrinkled and a sad expression turned down the corners of her mouth. "Yes, Rachel, it was. At least some of it. Other things that happened during those years made me very happy." Her thoughts turned to Four Horns, her husband of not quite two years.

"Like what?"

Touched by the child's innocence and trust, Rebecca searched her memory store for colorful images that would please Rachel. "Like every spring there would be clouds of butterflies that swayed and danced in the air. The buttercups and prairie rose, lupine, and other flowers bloomed in so many colors there weren't names for them all. Or in winter, rabbits dancing on the ice-capped snow in the moonlight. I was too old to play the little girl games, but I made dolls for some of the Oglala girls. They used to make tiny sleds for them and pull their favorites around the village. In summer, when the heat felt like a heavy blanket pushing down on you, we'd cool off by swimming in the Little White River. Or in a lake up in the Black Hills."

"Were there dances? I mean ones that girls could do?"

"Oh, yes. The Oglala love to dance. Girls did the basket dance and the weavers' dance, the fresh grass dance, and a lot of others. Little boys did the rabbit dance, the hunt dance, the Spirit Hawk dance, and of course, the war dance. Only theirs was over a pretend battle."

"It sounds fun."

"It was!" Rebecca burst out, full of enthusiasm. Then she

39

sobered. "At first, I didn't like it. Then, after I learned the language and made some friends it got to be . . . different."

"Miss Hawthorne said we have to have school every day while we're gone so we won't forget who we are."

"Miss Hawthorne," Rebecca started sharply, then moderated her tone. "Miss Hawthorne is a teacher, dear. Naturally she wants to help. School will keep all of you busy part of the day. That way time will travel fast."

"Will we really be set free?"

"I promise that you will. You'll all go back to your families."

"What about Tommy Archer? He doesn't want to go back."

Rebecca gave that a little thought. "Tommy is still a little boy. He may think he's been adopted as an Oglala, but that's not yet the case. By the time we're ready to take you back, he might find it much more desirable to come along."

"If he's a little boy, you can make him go," Rachel stated with the positiveness of a child.

"Not among the Oglala. Little boys rank just under big men. What women might think is right, or what they want, isn't always what they get."

Rachel's eyes grew large and round. "You mean he could stay?"

"Provided someone wanted him enough. Some man."

"Like Two Bulls?"

"Yes, or some other warrior who had lost a boy child to sickness or accident. The key is that someone has to *want* him badly. Tommy's full of enough mischief that he just might wear out his welcome."

Rachel giggled. "I've got to go now. Miss Hawthorne and her school. Do Oglala girls go to school?"

"Uh . . . no. No, they don't. Well, sort of a school. They learn to cook and sew and do beadwork, how to work quills into moccasins, to scrape hides for replacements on the lodge, make tools from bone."

"Is it hard?"

"Yes," Rebecca replied, remembering. "From before dawn

40

until after dark, Oglala women and girls have work to do. The play comes only when there's time. Now, you can't get around Miss Hawthorne by asking me more questions. Scoot."

"Yes, ma'am."

At the night stop, nine of the children gathered around Rebecca to listen to stories of life in an Oglala camp. Sally Hawthorne looked on and smoldered. Her resentment hung heavy in the air, like an odorous, unwashed blanket. Rebecca and Mrs. Stubens, an older woman, had taken to dealing with the youngsters' needs, comforting them. Sally Hawthorne wanted discipline and order, and they handed out hugs and reassurances. The effectiveness of the differing methods quickly became obvious.

It was difficult for Rebecca to extricate herself from her circle of curious boys and girls. Though the size of the gathering varied, it never failed to materialize right after the evening meal and chores. Once free of them, she found time to be alone with Whirlwind.

"You grow more beautiful every day," he whispered into her ear as they lay that night in a hollow-cut bank along the creek close to the camp.

"And you sound like a real suitor every night," Rebecca teased back.

She felt his body respond to her sensuous touch. A shock of delight bolted through Whirlwind as his flesh made contact with Rebecca's warm, soft lips.

Heat built and radiated from Whirlwind's body. The heady woman scent of her so close to his nose addled his wits. A groan began deep inside and he let it course outward. With both strong hands on her hips, he positioned Rebecca atop him.

Rebecca shivered at the delicious physical sensations. In so short a time he had mastered her body, arousing her to the ultimate heights of passion.

Reason fled Rebecca's mind in the overwhelming magnificence of the ecstasy they created together. Tugging and pulling, she worked furiously to draw Whirlwind to the edge of

41

completion, only to slack off and hold him in jittery suspense before starting over again. Inflamed, he repaid her for his joy, filling her with wave after wave of purest delight. Their pleasure continued through long minutes, past a quarter-hour and yet onward, before at last they succumbed to the inevitable and crashed groaning, completely exhausted.

The morning cookfires still smoldered in the circle of lodges when the warriors and their captives crested the rim of the shallow, dish-shaped valley. Children ran yelling and naked around the village. Older boys watched the pony herd and exchanged pleasant insults. From a long distance, the *eyanpaha* noted their arrival and mounted his droop-necked pony to perform his most frequent duty as camp crier.

"Hiewo! Hiewo! They come, they come! Our warriors are returning," he announced as he rode the concentric rings of buffalo hide lodges.

A great crowd formed behind him and made a procession of it, so that by the time he and the day's elected peace chief— head of the warrior society who were serving as *akicita,* the camp police—waited at the open eastern end of the encampment, everyone not involved with important duties elsewhere had gathered to welcome the arriving party. The children giggled, then shrieked in surprise and hid behind their mothers' skirts at the sight of so many white ones. Several pointed with stubby fingers, though that was rude, at a pale-haired boy who rode at the head of the column, between Two Bulls and Big Nose.

Despite loud protestations from Sally Hawthorne, Tommy Archer had taken this place of honor at the request of the war leader, Two Bulls. He sat proudly erect, his face alight with wonder and difficultly suppressed amazement. Lads his own age hollered at him with a jumble of insults.

"Why are you dressed as a Dakota?" one jeered.

"Do you have anything under that loincloth?" queried another. "Or are you really a girl?"

"Are you a half-breed? Your skin is too dark for a *wasicun*

42

and too light for an Oglala."

Tommy had made good use of his language lessons and startled the youngsters into big-eyed silence with his jesting replies. "I am called Mahtociquala. I dress like this because I am Dakota." Then he grabbed himself in the crotch so as to form a big bundle and added, "I've got more under here than any of you and I can prove it."

"*Unkce!*" spat the boy who had taunted him.

"Shit to you, too," Tommy sizzled back, reverting to English. Boylike, he had delighted in learning the dirty words first.

That brought cheery laughter from everyone. Not threatened by a possible future round of show-and-tell, some of the younger boys began to chant.

"*Tanka Ce, tanka Ce, tanka Ce!*"

Big Dingus, huh, Tommy thought. It might not be too accurate, but at least he didn't need a tweezer to find it. He swelled his chest and gave a particularly winning grin to a boy of about his own age who rushed forward to greet Whirlwind with the cry of "Brother!"

"Is that your kid brother?" Tommy asked over his shoulder to Tatekohom'ni.

An answering smile flashed white teeth in Whirlwind's face. "Yes, it is. I hope you'll be friends."

"Oh, I reckon so," Tommy replied in a mixture of English and Lakota. "He's one of the few who didn't make insults."

Big Nose uttered a bark of laughter. "They insult you because they like you, like your style."

"That's a funny way of showing it."

"That's the Oglala way, Mahtociquala."

When the fuss over their arrival ended, Rebecca spoke earnestly to Ptasan Okiye. "I speak as a daughter of this band, Ptasan Okiye. Much trouble could come from taking hostages, especially children."

"It was not my thought to do so, Šinaskawin. Two Bulls acted on his own, as is his right as war leader. The council

43

approved the carrying of the pipe of war for this one raid to open the white soldiers' eyes."

"It will more than open them, White Buffalo Helps Him. The *wasicun* take the stealing of children quite seriously. They're quick to anger and slow to talk peace."

"*Ho.* We'll speak of this with the council. Come this way."

Seven clan chiefs met in the council lodge. Their faces grave, they listened to Rebecca's impassioned explanation of why the white children must be returned immediately. When she concluded, the leader of the Water Bird clan rose and touched the pipe.

"Before we consider this path, I would first ask Sinaskawin on what side she will stand?"

Although rude by Sioux custom, the question had been spoken, its import out in the open, and none spoke to call it back. With hope sinking for the first time, Rebecca realized she had a great deal of trouble on her hands.

Chapter 5

"We will speak on that tomorrow," Ptasan Okiye announced, saving Rebecca the difficulty of answering at once. "There is feasting to be held for our warriors; those who fell are to be remembered and grieved. We'll let this matter wait until these are done. Go now, child," he said in a kindly tone to Rebecca, "find those of your family who are among us and seek acquaintances to share their food bowls at the feast."

"Thank you, Grandfather," Rebecca replied politely. Then she made her way out of the lodge, careful to walk on the woman's side of the fire.

A chubby young woman with a full-moon face, greeted her first when she left the council lodge. "Šinaskawin! It's really you!" A frown furrowed the lunar smoothness when she received no immediate reaction. "I'm Blue Willow. Surely you remember?"

"Oh, of course. But you were . . . just a girl."

"I'm the mother of two now. And happy. Like you and . . . I'm happy with my family."

"I hope you have all the happiness Four Horns and I had," Rebecca replied tactfully.

"Thank you, Šinaskawin," Blue Willow effused, relieved that her near slip had been forgiven. "You came with the white captives? Is that right?"

"It's true enough. Only I hope to soon have them considered as guests, rather than captives."

Blue Willow made a grimace. "Oh, Šinaskawin, you're forever making things happen. I used to envy you so."

"It's my turn to thank you. Have you seen Rainbow or Shining Woman?"

"Yes, they're over preparing dog stew for the feast. They'll be so glad to see you. Especially if you can do something about that little white Oglala boy who keeps pestering them."

"Tommy Archer? What is he, ah, Mahtociquala, doing to bother the women who are cooking?"

"There are four buffalo calves roasting on spits. When the women get busy, and they aren't watching, he sneaks up and cuts strips of the cooking meat for the other boys."

"That sounds like Small Bear, all right," Rebecca agreed. "Come along and I'll see what can be done."

"Ow!" Tommy Archer cried out when Rebecca Caldwell caught him by the ear.

"Listen to me, you little jackanapes," she said rapidly in English. "I'm going to give you a good piece of hell about bothering around these fires in Lakota so the other boys can understand a lesson in manners. They usually turn campfire robbers over to the little girls to torture, they being the lowest form of life and beneath the attention of warriors. In case you can't follow what I'm going to say, that's the essence of it."

Quickly she assailed him with rippling syllables of Lakota. As she spoke, black-haired heads popped out from several hiding places. Eyes growing large as she detailed the nature of the supposed tortures, the suddenly solemn little boys groped self-consciously at their crotches, vicariously feeling the loss of what they already considered their symbols of superiority over the girls, who had only an unhealed wound where a *ce* should have been.

"So get on out of here quickly, before I set the little girls on you," Rebecca concluded.

The last dark head of the wild pack had hardly disappeared

around a distant tipi when the women began to giggle. A couple of the older ladies brayed with toothless laughter.

"'Cut it off and dry it like a buffalo pizzel,'" a fat matron chortled, repeating one of Rebecca's more colorful quotes. "You're the best at turning the air blue, Šinaskawin. How do you ever come up with all those things?"

"I've been among the white folks, remember? That gives a person lots of room to grow her imagination."

"You will eat with our family at the feast?"

"No, eat with ours," urged another woman.

"I'll eat with you both, and thank you for your hospitality. Is there anything I can do to help?"

"No," they all assured her. "You are a guest this time."

Rebecca made her way through the circles of lodges, greeting those she had known from before. An old man came to her, back bowed with the weight of his years, thin skin drawn taut over the bones, his voice quavery.

"They called you Becky when you first came to us many summers ago," he blurted in fits and starts. "But I know you. You are Šinaskawin, *cunks* of Iron Calf." He raised a spidery hand in a gesture of rejection. "Oh, I know, he's with the Spirits and it's not polite to speak his name, but he was a great chief and you are a beautiful daughter. You are welcome here."

How welcome would she be after tomorrow, Rebecca wondered, and said, "Thank you, Grandfather."

Not the least put off by the prospect of icy cold water this late in fall, the recently chastised boys streamed across the lush brown grass of the valley to the creek. They sought out their favorite spot, a wide bend that made a deep pool below a high bank on one side. Tommy Archer and several of the white captive boys went along. Tommy found the smiling lad from that morning beside him.

"The sun smiles on you, Small Bear," the youngster said shyly.

47

"You're Whirlwind's brother, eh? What are you called?" Tommy asked.

The boy blushed. "Tipsila Ce."

"I know what a *ce* is," Tommy replied, himself turning pink. "What is *tipsila?*"

"Turnip," the boy answered in a low voice.

"Why do they call you that?"

"When we get to the swimming place, you'll see," he answered miserably.

With a yell of delight, the boys reached their goal. Tommy Archer and Tipsila Ce stripped out of their moccasins and loincloths like the others. When they did, Tipsila Ce revealed the shortest, fattest male member Tommy had ever seen.

"Uh, gosh," Tommy blurted out, uncertain what to say. "Does it . . . ah, does it ever get any bigger?"

"A little bit. When I, well, you know. Mostly, though, it only gets fatter. My father introduced me to the Great Spirit as Capa. My uncle, Running Horse, thought it would be funny, so he started calling me Turnip Penis, instead of Beaver. The name, ah, stuck."

Despite himself, Tommy broke out in a grin. "That's not so bad," he philosophized. "I'm not really all that great a shakes, as you can see."

"Sometimes I just want to die," Tipsila Ce returned vehemently.

"How many summers do you have?"

"Ten."

"Then what's to worry about? You'll grow. Wait and see."

"You two! Did you come here to talk or to swim?" a commanding voice called from the creek. "Get in the water."

With a friendly wave, Tommy shouted back. "We're coming." To his new friend he added, "Someday you'll show 'em all up. Until then, do you want me to call you Capa?"

"Would you? That'd be wonderful."

Together they dived awkwardly into the water.

*   *   *

Cottonwood and blackjack pine painted long black fingers on the buffalo grass, and the lowering sun made orange paths between them. The calls of night birds began to replace those of their daytime brothers. Clusters of the Šayaota gathered around cooking fires, as several families would gather to celebrate the achievements of their participants in the raid on the train. For the most part, their talk was gay, and much laughter rose. Only those with men missing from a family lodge restrained themselves.

Because of this, it turned out not to be a general feasting. Not every grouping, or even clan, took part. There were enough gatherings though to provide a party atmosphere.

The air, redolent with the savory odor of roasted meat and piquant stews, seemed nonetheless pleasant for the chill it bore. The children ganged together to add shrill accompaniment to the chatter of the women and the quiet talk of the men. Although technically captives themselves, Rebecca and Lone Wolf visited several of these clusters of relatives and enjoyed a bowl of the offered fare. Then darkness came, with uncustomary suddenness. Thick black storm clouds blocked off the distant view of the sacred Black Hills. The old men heaped more wood on the central fire and people began to gather. The drum thumped in a heartbeat rhythm and the warriors began to recount their exploits.

Each one had a different, intricate step that he incorporated into his dance, and their singsong voices chanted the number of arrows or bullets they had fired, the white men they had killed, wounded or counted *coup* upon. The last to dance into the ring and join the shuffling performers was the youngest, Whirlwind.

"Three times one hand, HO! Three times one hand, HO! The arrows sped swift and true from my bow. Three times one hand, HO! Two times one hand, HEYA! Two times one hand, HEYA! Bullets crashed from my gun. See the white breath of the iron horse. See the white breath come from its belly. My bullets went true. Two times one hand, HEYA! A black-coat iron-horse man holds his shoulder and bleeds while I count

49

coup. A funny-looking white man falls down as though dead before I can touch him. I fired the first arrow and shot the last ball. The fight ended. I have spoken."

With three braves dead and five seriously wounded, there were few in the mood for social dancing, which usually followed the warriors' legends. The little girls formed a circle and stamped around the fire in a graceful friendship dance and drew two of the captive children in with them. Then they summoned Rebecca, who dutifully joined in. As a feast it didn't rate as much. Everyone was asleep before the moon rose to bathe the valley in orange harvest light.

"The Sky Father is hardly out of his sleeping robes," Two Bellies complained good-naturedly as he stooped to enter the council lodge.

"You are last to arrive, as usual," White Buffalo Helps Him informed the aged counselor. Then he went on to explain the situation that had brought surprise to the eyes of Two Bellies.

"Śinaskawin is a true daughter of our band and of our former chief. She is also a warrior woman by right and deed. She's avenged herself and our people many times against evil white men and earned her place here. Today she sits in this council."

"I am honored, Grandfather," Rebecca replied humbly.

When the summons had come with daylight, Rebecca had not been able to hide her amazement. What had happened since the previous day to change the humor of the council and its leader, the Civil Chief, Ptasan Okiye? No matter, the council had spoken and she would obey. Now she arranged her skirt about her knees, seated as were the men, cross-legged on a comfortable pile of buffalo robes. A low fire crackled in the stone ring at the center of the tipi, its flames reflected in the expressionless obsidian eyes of the council.

"We must speak of the white women and children brought here," White Buffalo began. "Although the idea has merit, it

50

wasn't done at our bidding. Two Bulls took it upon himself to do this thing. We must approve or reject it. How do my counselors feel about this?"

Pro and con, the arguments went on for a long hour. By tradition, Rebecca refrained from touching the pipe to signify she wished to speak until all others had had their say. Then she leaned over and laid her small, well-formed hand on the carved wooden stem. Her black tresses glowed in tight braids as she rose to speak. They sky leaped from her startlingly deep blue eyes.

"What has been said is wise, Ptasan Okiye. Each man here has spoken his heart. There's strength and truth on both sides. Thus it would be seen by our people. Yet of all who are here, I alone have dwelled among the white men. I know also their ways. By their lights, what's been done is wrong. They're not inclined to be lenient in matters involving their women or children. This my white side tells me.

"But my heart is Oglala and it tells me that what Two Bulls did was necessary. It will get the white soldier chief's attention. If the children and the three women are returned unharmed, it will show your hearts are for peace. Yet, none will doubt the strength of the Oglala. Someone must carry this message to the white fort." Here she paused a long while to let the idea soak in before launching into her main proposal.

"If you would permit me, I would serve as a peace emissary to the Army and the Territorial Government. Speak with them in their tongue. As a sign of good faith, I should take the captives back with me. This way everyone can find an accommodation suitable to them in the making of a new agreement. I have spoken."

"This cannot be!" Black Cloud thundered after touching the pipe. "The soldiers will not attack so long as we hold their young. They will make talk and bring the words on paper, exchange gifts. Then, after more talk, they will take the children away and we will have peace . . . for only so long as it pleases them. I have spoken."

Two Bulls touched the pipe. "The white children weren't any trouble on the way here. Many who rode with my war pipe became their friends. There are none of us who want to harm them. If the soldiers and the white men in long coats do not hear our words, what then? Do we kill these young ones? Do we make them into slaves? My heart is heavy and I don't have the words. I have spoken."

Considerable grumbling followed, each man feeling bound to represent his clan and its interests. Those who had lost warriors in the raid demanded some compensation. Two Bulls said simply that they had wrecked the train and cost the white men much of the yellow metal they prized so highly. Wasn't that enough? Others added their words. At last the council listened to a summation by White Buffalo Helps Him, and then the decision was made.

Rebecca would be their peace commissioner. She would take the children back to the place called Camp Cullen and talk with the soldier chief. She would also talk with the whites who came from the Great White Father. Two Bulls rose at the end of this announcement.

"Someone should go with her to protect so many helpless ones and make sure the white soldiers understand the seriousness of the situation."

Mutters of agreement went the rounds.

"How many?" White Buffalo inquired.

"Too many would make them think we came for war. Too few," Two Bellies offered, "could fall to a Crow war party or would make them think they could punish us by killing them and taking the children."

"A party of five or six would show strength and make the Absaroka cautious," Rebecca suggested.

Agreement quickly followed and Ptasan Okiye summoned the camp crier to announce this expedition. Within moments a familiar voice sounded from outside the lodge.

"I will go," Whirlwind declared. "I wish to see the funny doings of the white men."

"I will also go," a soprano voice chirped. "The white soldiers will know we come in peace if a boy like Tipsila Ce is along."

A ripple of laughter went around the council.

"I, too, would like to see the antics of the white men," White Buffalo announced. "Besides, it is well known that the whites like to talk to a chief."

That remark elicited a round of hearty laughter. Everyone knew that the whites thought that a chief had absolute authority. Whoever would want such an absurdity? The council ended and they all went outside where the remainder of the party was quickly selected. They would depart the next morning at first light.

Chapter 6

Like a dust storm in high summer, the miasma churned up by thirty-one horses could be marked for a long distance over the rolling prairie of Dakota Territory. Lt. Arnulf Larsen sat his roan mount and watched the progress, on a diagonal course to that of his column. It couldn't be the hostiles they sought, he reasoned. If they maintained that direction, they'd come to Camp Cullen.

"Dismount the troops, Sergeant," he commanded.

"Sir, yes, sir. Prepare to dismount . . . Dis-mount!"

"Sergeant Thompkins. Have the men brew coffee, but make sure it's a smokeless fire. We don't want to attract the attention of any hostiles."

"Yer right on that, sir," Thompkins acknowledged. With a less-than-parade-ground salute, he turned to the men. "Coffee time, lads. But use buffalo chips, no campfire smoke for this one."

"The men may use tobacco if they wish, Sergeant," Larsen said.

Larsen bided a long fifteen minutes, much to the relief of his saddle-sore troopers, watching the distant movement of the cloud of dust. The rain that had threatened on the previous night had not materialized, much to his relief. Had it come this late in the year, it would most certainly have contained sleet.

55

An ice storm in the field he could do without.

With a languid motion, Larsen produced his pocket watch and checked the time. "Off and on, Sergeant Thompkins. We'll leave in five minutes. That hostile camp can't be far from here."

"How you figure that, sir? Beggin' the lieutenant's pardon, sir, but the scouts haven't reported back anything about a camp."

"I know, Sergeant. All the same, this looks like good country for a big village. I've a hunch we're within half a day's ride."

Thompkins grinned. "Yer gettin' better'n all those buckskin civilians we've got hired, sir. A reg'lar eagle-eye."

"Are you buttering me up, Sergeant?"

"Ah, me, sir? Oh, no, sir. I meant that as a sincere compliment. Ain't many who could pick up on trail savvy fast as you have, sir."

"Then, thank you, Sergeant. Have the men tighten their girths and we'll ride out."

Around midafternoon, Tommy Archer, Chad Bennett, and Tipsila Ce were seized with a sudden fit of giggles. Rebecca Caldwell could not determine the cause. A scant five minutes after their outburst, the trio declared they were riding ahead to look for Lone Wolf, who scouted for the column, and drummed their horses to a lope.

Once out of sight of the string of children and braves, the lads reined in. "It's right over there. A big buffalo wallow," Tipsila Ce informed his friends. "This is the Moon of Cold Rains. There will be much water."

"Yeah. And lots of frogs," Chad Bennett said wistfully in English.

When Tommy translated this to Tipsila Ce, the boys broke out in giggles again. The Oglala boy waved them forward with his arm and they trotted off through the shoulder-high brown grass, wrapped in their own thoughts. Cresting a swale, they

56

looked down on a large round pond, sunlight winking off a respectable expanse of water. The gumbo mud edges showed the marks of many animals, mostly buffalo, but coyote, racoon, and antelope as well. The boys brought their horses down and halted at the blasted stumps of a lightning-struck cottonwood. There they tied them off.

Chad had taken to wearing a loincloth and moccasins also and had no more difficulty than the other boys in removing his garments. The trio waded their ungainly way out through the thick, wet mud, which squished between their bare toes and turned them dark chocolate to the knees.

"We'll swim for a while first, then catch frogs," Tommy declared.

Although a year older, Chad accepted Tommy as a natural leader. He grinned his agreement and made a shallow dive into the icy water.

"Yeeow!" he shrieked when he surfaced.

Laughing and shouting, the other two joined him. The serious part of their dereliction began twenty minutes later. Once satisfied with their catch, they rubbed the sun-dried mud from their feet and legs, redressed and rode off, a curiously lively gunnysack bouncing on the rump of Tommy's pony.

Evening camp had been made and the meal eaten in relative peace. Throughout the day, Rebecca had found her patience wearing thin with Whirlwind's little brother. Tipsila Ce was another Tommy Archer, from a darker mold. Tommy had solemnly declared that he was not going back. That he was going to tell the soldiers that he wanted to stay with the Oglala. *His* stubbornness had been trying enough. Then there had been the secret of their afternoon departure. Something unpleasant, she felt sure, would come of it.

Sudden shrieks and squeals from the girls in the camp vindicated her suspicion. Rachel Tilton came to her on the run, screaming as she churned her short, pudgy legs.

"Oh, Rebecca, Rebecca, they . . . they dumped *frogs* on us! It's awful. Those terrible, nasty boys."

"What frogs?" Rebecca inquired, though she felt certain she had uncovered the secret of the moving gunnysack. "Which boys?"

"Tommy Archer, and Chad Bennett, an' that Tipsi—Tipsi . . ."

"Tipsila Ce," Rebecca completed. "I suspected as much. Now slow down and tell me all about it."

"We were washing our hands and faces at the creek," Rachel began, still panting from excitement and exertion. "Martha, and Lenore, and Miss Hawthorne and me. We-we, well, we waded in a bit, under the screen of some willows. Then it started to rain f-f-frogs. Ugh! Such awful creatures. All slimy and ugly and scary."

Damn, a little of that sort of thing went a long way, Rebecca thought. Yet she couldn't help but bend a fleeting smile, visualizing the frenzy of frightened females, the flash of indelicately exposed limbs, flying water, and a downpour of croaking, confused frogs.

"Which do you mean, dear? The frogs or the boys are awful creatures?"

"The frogs. No, the boys." Aware she was being teased, Rachel's terror turned to anger. Hands on hips, she stamped a foot. "Both of them."

"Well, you wait right here, Rachel. We'll see what we can do about this."

Lone Wolf and Whirlwind rounded up the errant youngsters and prodded them to the fireside. Chad Bennett looked chagrined. His sun-browned belly, spotted with the pink of sunburn, protruded slightly over the thong of his loincloth, with the last vestige of baby-fat. Lean and brown as a rawhide whiplash, Tommy Archer stood hipshot, his bare legs slightly apart, head turned downward, though more to hide the gleam of mischief in his blue eyes than in contrition. Tipsila Ce, square and blocky, grinned like a cream-fed cat. It had been a wonderful adventure. They all agreed on that.

"You boys have done a low, mean thing," Rebecca lectured

them, first in English, for the benefit of the audience that had gathered, then in Lakota. "You frightened Miss Hawthorne and these girls and nearly caused them to get soaking wet. In this weather they could catch their death of lung fever."

"White women are too delicate," Tipsila Ce said softly, his eyes studying the toes of his moccasins.

"Never mind that," Rebecca snapped, her endurance—at least for this day—worn to a shadow. "The point is that we have to get along and reach our destination sound in body and looking clean as possible."

"I don't wanna go at all," Tommy Archer protested. "My dad ran away from the fight, my mom clings on me like a tick an' won't let me have any fun, and I hate my little sister. Capa is my brother now," he went on, calling Tipsila Ce Beaver as he had promised.

The boys draped arms around each other's shoulders. Even Chad moved closer and took Tommy by the hand. If she pushed this too hard, Rebecca realized, she'd have another one demanding to live among the Oglala.

"I want a promise from each one of you that you won't do something like this again."

"That's not enough," Sally Hawthorne blustered. "These little—little heathens deserve a royal switching. They should be spanked until their, ah, bottoms glow."

"I'm afraid you'd be defeating your purpose, Miss Hawthorne," Rebecca answered tactfully. "Boys their ages are beyond the benefits of a sound spanking, and Oglala children are never given physical punishment."

"Then this pernicious savage is about to learn all about it," Sally countered in high dudgeon.

Rebecca shook her head sadly. "I'm sorry, but no. If you were to try it, our 'friendly' escorts would most likely lift your hair. They don't take kindly to other people, particularly white, female people, breaking their customs and taboos."

Sally blanched. Her lip trembling in righteous indignation, she demanded hotly, "You mean you—you'd let them get

59

away with this outrage?"

"Oh, not at all. For the rest of the journey they'll be digging and filling in the sanitary pits."

A chorus of groans answered her.

"No 'ooohs' about it. I mean that, boys. Or would you rather I had Ptasan Okyie order you to do it?"

That they knew would mean some pulled ears and a lot of scathing, insulting remarks. Slowly they shook their heads in the negative.

"We'll be good, Miss Rebecca, I promise," Chad forced out a low voice, heavy with contrition.

"Does that go for all of you?"

"Stop it! Stop this farce," Sally Hawthorne shouted nastily. "I demand that they be strapped. Did you hear, I *demand* it."

Rebecca smiled sweetly and stepped closer to the raging woman. "You're not in any position to demand anything. This boy," and she pointed to Tommy, "has been adopted into Two Bulls's family. It was done with ritual, according to their customs, to replace a younger brother whom Two Bulls dearly loved. He's Oglala now. If you looked into it, I'm certain one or more of these men escorting us would be willing to say the same for Chad. If you did something to offend them, there's nothing short of killing them that we could do to stop their revenge. Technically, you are still a hostage. Do you need to be told what the Sioux traditionally do to women hostages?"

Sally Hawthorne's eyes rolled upward and she swayed dizzily. "Y-you'd ne-never allow it!" she wailed. "I—I . . . It's inhuman."

"And it happens every day. Now get one thing straight, Miss Hawthorne. You are a hostage and I'm here to see you get safely back to civilization. You do not demand, you do not order, you do not do anything but what you are told. Once we are at Camp Cullen, you can do or say anything you want. Until then, for your own sake, be careful."

It had taken enormous effort for Sally to regain her usual composure. "Are you quite through?"

"I am," Rebecca replied mildly. "I'm not sure *they* are."

For the first time, Sally looked at the menacing ring of warriors who surrounded them, scowls deep on their faces. She realized that all the while that terrible old man, White Buffalo, had been translating everything being said to his fellow savages. She began to tremble.

"D-don't let them . . . don't l-leave me t-t-to them. . . ." she stammered.

"*Ta ta iciya wo*, she understands," Rebecca said to the men. "Relax," she told them again. Then to Sally, "You should do the same."

Later, in the quiet of the midnight hour, as Rebecca and Whirlwind lay in each other's arms under the stars, he murmured a compliment into her ear. "You did just right with the boys. They're wild sparks; still, to quench them with cold water would leave you no fire in the morning."

"You are being philosophical tonight," she told him, using the English word.

"What is philosophical?"

"*Taku śkanśkan*."

"Ummh. I see."

Rebecca suppressed a tinkle of laughter. "From what I'm feeling pressed against my stomach, you aren't just *spiritually* vital. Oh! Oh, Whirlwind, that's nice. Yes, do that. Again. So good.

They were swept by waves of passion, locked in each other's arms, and the night sped blissfully by.

Twisted Foot had chosen the site well for the nine lodges that followed him. Although old, and unable to lead the hunt any longer, Twisted Foot retained the respect of his sons and their wives, his cousin Fat Elk and the many children of their small band. They had left the big hoop of the Red Top Lodges three summers ago, after the Sun Dance and before the fight on the Greasy Grass. Twisted Foot would not go to the reservation, yet in all other ways he walked the path of the white man's choosing. In the cold, predawn hours, two of those white men sat in judgment on the future of Twisted Foot and his band.

"You reckon there's anything worth takin' down there?" Aaron Carter asked in a whisper. His long, yellow-streaked, baby-fine, sandy brown hair swayed in a nimbus around his large head, pushed by a random breeze. Unconsciously, he rubbed at the purplish "strawberry" birthmark behind his right ear.

"Don't be so coarse, Carter," Branch Delano answered back. "There's nothing any unbaptized redskin savage would have that could interest me. After some of the reports I've heard of looting, that's why I came along on this raid. You and the other range detectives are supposed to drive these heathen scum out, not plunder them like the pirates of old."

Carter snorted derisively and peered through the weakness of starlight at his companion. At forty-five, Branch Delano remained solidly built, keen of eye, and able to sit a saddle for long hours at a time. Carter recognized that the brown-eyed, quick-tempered cattleman had more than the typical hatred of Indians. Something to do with his wife, he understood.

"Yer no better or worse'n I am, Mr. Delano. Yer idea of drivin' 'em out is to kill off the women and youngin's and leave the bucks to be yer enemies."

"'Root and branch,' Carter. 'Root and branch.' Or as General Sherman put it, 'nits make lice.' It's our bounden duty as Christians to rid this land of these children of Satan. We're doing the work of the Lord this night."

"Way I see it," Aaron Carter returned through a squirt of tobacco juice, "long's I'm gettin' paid for it, it's work worth doin', no matter who's the boss."

"Do not blasapheme, Carter. *He* might be listening. I wouldn't want you going home decorated up as a pin cushion for Sioux arrows."

"No fear o' that, Mr. Delano. You yourself said God was on

our side, right?"

"Don't get impertinent, Carter. I could arrange to have you removed as chief of the regulators. Now let's go kill us some Sioux."

Twisted Foot stirred, restless in the light sleep of the aged. Were those buffalo he heard pounding over the ground? Were the hunters streaming along the sides of the herd, bows poised and arrows ready to sink into the pounding hearts and bellows lungs of the mighty beasts? The sound seemed to grow closer.

"*Waaguh!*" came a startled shout from the lodge next to his. "*Waśicun, waśicun! Takpeyapo!*"

White men? Attacking us? The thoughts swirled mistily in Twisted Foot's head. How could this be? He had the big peace medallion from the Great White Father. What white men?

Death thundered through the small ring of lodges. Women screamed and children howled in terror as six-guns and carbines blazed into the night. Twisted Foot's wife, old, gray, and lined like himself, huddled in one corner of the lodge while her husband found his Remington rolling block and started out the door of the lodge.

A blast of .00 buckshot slammed Twisted Foot back inside. Flames began to flicker among the lodges. A frightened child ran from a burning tipi, to be clubbed down with a rifle butt and trampled under the milling hoofs of a dozen horses. Another youngster loosed an arrow from his rabbit bow. Driven by a forty-pound pull, the short, stone-barbed shaft sank deeply into the fat-larded belly of a range detective.

Squealing like a pig at butcher time, the man dropped his revolver and clutched at the wiggling projectile, the fletchings crushed by his big hands. A pitiful expression came on his face and he blanched white before he sagged to one side, shock graying his flesh as he slid from the saddle.

Quickly the little boy ran forward with his knife and began to peel away the scalp lock. His victim howled in anguish and

63

struck weakly at the lad. Nimbly, he jumped away, only to have his small head exploded like a gourd by a big lead slug from Branch Delano's .45 Colt

"Good work, boys," Delano declared loudly. "Now let's get out of here."

Only a handful, eight pitiful survivors, remained after the white men rode off into the darkness. Sobbing and wailing in grief, they examined the carnage by the light of their burning lodges.

Chapter 7

It hadn't rained since before the grass had been burned off around the outpost. To Maj. Ed Varney, the adjutant at Camp Cullen, the blackened expanse looked like a landscape out of the Inferno. Viewed from above it would have had the appearance of a giant bull's eye, with the post as the "X" ring. Worse, the incessant wind blew the sticky black ash into every crevice and cranny. It clung to rifles, uniforms, bedding, cooking utensils, to anything where it was unwelcome.

Another of Bryce Peyton's follies, Varney thought. Although he liked the commander of Camp Cullen, considered himself a friend, Ed Varney had to admit that Peyton's obsession with "punishing" the Indians for the "massacre" of Georgie Custer and his men frequently got in the way of properly running a military post. Varney stood alone on the narrow rampart above the main gate—an affectation, since the palisade only surrounded three sides of the cantonment. Breakfast sat like a leaden lump in his stomach and he bided time before officers' call with a smoke and a bit of gazing into the distance.

It was his sharp, clear eyes, then, that first picked out the approaching riders. Three of them. White men from the way they sat their mounts, their hats and the flopping side panels of their coats. Varney turned away and started for the ladder when the sentry sang out.

"Corporal of the Guard, Post Number Two! Riders approaching."

If it had been the Sioux, Varney thought uncharitably, they would have been on the parade ground before the front gate could be closed. When had it become practice, he wondered, to have those with the worst eyesight assigned to sentry duty? He clambered down to the ground and straightened his uniform in time to greet the visitors.

"Mr. Carmoody, Mr. Ridgeway, a good morning to you. And, ah, who's this gentleman with you?"

"Hello, Varney," Carmoody replied stiffly. "This is Branch Delano, another member of the Association."

"Mr. Delano. What brings you three out this way?"

"Came to see Bryce," Carmoody clipped off shortly.

Inwardly Varney winced at this familiarity. He had to remind himself that Carmoody was a civilian and a longtime friend of Bryce Peyton's. The lack of military address in Carmoody's remarks only reflected the typical civilian contempt for those in uniform.

"It's about time for officers' call, but I think he can take time to make you comfortable until that's over," Varney responded at last, forcing a heartiness into his voice that he didn't feel.

"Good enough. Would you have a boy take care of our horses?"

"This isn't . . ." Varney started in sharp retort, then calmed, sensitive to the relationship between the powerful cattleman and his superior officer. "There isn't anyone usually detailed for that. Leave them at the tie-rail in front of headquarters and I'll see what Sergeant Major Roach can arrange."

"Thank you," Carmoody replied with a hint of amusement.

He'd been right, Varney thought, the bastard enjoyed baiting soldiers. Stiff-legged, he led the way across the parade to the headquarters building. Once again, Carmoody managed to upstage him, acting as though the sentry's salute was meant for

66

him instead of a major in uniform.

"That's all right, sonny. No need for all the fluff and feathers for me," Carmoody boomed in artificial good humor as the guard raised his hand to his rifle in salute.

Inside, his thunderous expression transmitted the mood to Sergeant Major Roach sufficiently for the senior NCO to grasp the situation instantly. Roach managed to keep Carmoody, Ridgeway, and Delano waiting an uncomfortably long time before admitting them to Colonel Peyton's office. After the door had closed behind their backs, Roach indicated them with a nod and a wink.

"That one's an arrogant son of a bitch, if you'll pardon my saying so, sir."

"No pardon needed, Sergeant Major. He's every bit of that, and more."

Carmoody received a warm, effusive welcome from Colonel Peyton. "Alystaire, it's good to see you again, You, too, Grover. I don't believe I've met you, sir."

"Branch Delano, from over White River way," Carmoody filled in.

"How do you do? Sit down, gentlemen."

"You're looking well, Bryce," Carmoody returned.

"Wish I felt that way. It's a bit early for brandy—would you care for coffee?"

"Yes, thank you," the ranchers replied.

Peyton crossed to a pewter coffee service, the pot being kept warm over a bottle that contained lumps of burning charcoal. He poured four cups, splashing cream into his visitors' and adding sugar to Carmoody's. He handed them out as he spoke again.

"What brings you to this desolate spot, Alystaire?"

Carmoody frowned. "The usual, Bryce. The damned Sioux."

Peyton nodded sagely. "I know what you mean. You heard about the attack on the Frisco daily, of course?"

"Damn me if that wasn't the limit," Carmoody thundered.

67

"Oh, it was, I assure you. I have one company out tracking the hostiles now. The other two are on alert and I've sent for the rest of the regiment. This time we're going to break their backs. Any of the vermin who survive will *beg* to be put on the reservation."

"Ought to shoot the lot of them," Delano growled.

"Now, now. That would never sit well with department headquarters or the sob-sisters back East."

"Bryce, you know this country has to open up to whites eventually. In the long run it doesn't matter what these putty-brained snivelers back in New York or even Washington think of how we deal with the savages."

"It does if you have a career to protect, Alystaire," Peyton returned dryly.

"This, ah, campaign of yours," Grover Ridgeway injected, drawing them back to the subject. "Have you cleared it with department headquarters?"

"Well, ah, not entirely. Colonel Johansen has authorized punitive measures against the hostiles who attacked the train, naturally. So far, that's all though."

Carmoody shrewdly studied his friend over the rim of his cup. "How far do you intend to go, Bryce?"

"Like I told you. I plan to go after the main bunch this time. The Red Top Lodge Oglala have been getting away with defiance for too long."

Eyes narrowed, Carmoody spoke slowly, his words heavy with his hate. "You spoke of those who'll survive being driven onto the reservation. I certainly hope that'll be confined to older persons, those beyond child-bearing age?"

For a moment, Bryce Peyton gave his visitors a bleak, scathing look. Then his features relaxed and a smile played about his lips. "That's my sincere intention. George Custer has got to be avenged. So far, damn-all little has been done about it. Outside of Nelson Miles's expedition in the winter of seventy-six/seventy-seven, show me one thing positive that has been

accomplished toward a final solution to the Indian question."
Warming to his favorite theme, Bryce Peyton waxed eloquent.
"The Cheyenne and Sioux are thumbing their noses at us.
They ride across the plains without the least pretense of
obeying regulations that require they stay on the agencies.
Why, even the Blackfoot, who have been accommodating in
the past, are working up toward some show of defiance. You'd
think this land was theirs, not ours. What we didn't win by
conquest, we acquired in the Louisiana Purchase more than
sixty years ago. The Indians simply have to accept that
fact . . . or be exterminated."

Eyes aglow with zeal, Branch Delano leaned forward in his
chair. "I like that last word."

"You sound like a man with a mission, Mr. Delano," Peyton
observed.

"I suppose that you could say that I am. My wife and I are
from Minnesota. We had a farm not far from the Sioux
reservation. Our children were born there, grew into their
teens. I-in sixty-two I was away fighting for the Union cause
w-when t-the Sioux went on the rampage. Little Crow led it,
you may recall. M-m-my wife has been a semi-invalid since. The
Sioux burned my barn, part of the house. Edyth was, ah, that is,
the savages h-h-had their way and then shot her in the back
with an arrow, left her for dead. My sons, fifteen and thirteen,
and a daughter, eleven, were, ah, misused also, then killed."

During the painful recounting, Bryce Peyton had come to
his feet and crossed the room to Delano's chair. He knelt beside
the man, a hand on the rancher's shoulder, tears streaming
down his cheeks.

"May God have mercy on you, my friend. And may He soon
bring recompense for all you and yours have suffered. You
have my sincerest condolences, Mr. Delano."

Profoundly moved by Branch Delano's story, Colonel Bryce

69

Peyton had not entirely regained his composure by mid-afternoon, when Sergeant Major Roach announced more visitors.

"A Mr. Baylor, Miss Caldwell, and two Sioux, sir," Roach informed him. "One of 'em's White Buffalo. I recognize him from the last attempt to put his band on the reservation, sir."

The damned impertinence of these savages, Peyton thought angrily. Call on the area military commander as though they had every right to walk around free. He scowled his disapproval and spoke.

"What do they want, Sergeant Major?"

"Sir, beggin' yer pardon, sir, but you're not gonna believe this. They brought back some women and children, sir. Claim they're from that Frisco train. Took 'em off the renegades who raided the train, they say, sir."

"What? Are you sure? What's your opinion, Sergeant Major?"

Roach pursed his lips, considered the appearance of the ragtag party that had appeared on the parade ground five minutes before. "Could be they're tellin' the truth. You ever heard of a man named Baylor before, sir?"

Colonel Peyton rubbed at his chin, thinking over the hundreds of names that had come to his attention over the years on the frontier. Vaguely, an image formed in his mind. There had been one man—he'd heard of him when he had first been assigned to the frontier, down in Nebraska. Captured by the Crow, the story went, then went on to become one of their fiercest warriors.

"His name again, Sergeant Major?"

"Baylor, sir. Brett Baylor."

"That's the one. A white renegade, by all accounts. Oh, this would have been fifteen, sixteen years ago. Taken by the Crow. And I know the story on the Caldwell woman. Given over to the Oglala as a girl." Peyton's fist slammed the desktop. "By God, it was the Red Top Lodge band, come to think of it. Iron Calf was war chief then. You say White Buffalo is with them? Let's have a look at 'em then, sergeant major."

"Yes, sir."

When the four persons had been shown in, Colonel Peyton offered chairs to Rebecca and Lone Wolf. Seeing that the others were being slighted, they refused, not too politely. Peyton scowled.

"I understand you claim to have brought back the women and children captured off the Frisco train," he began icily. .

"We have," Rebecca responded. "Mr. Baylor and I were passengers when the raid happened. We were at last able to talk the war party into surrendering their captives. Actually," she embroidered the facts slightly, "White Buffalo Helps Him was instrumental in our being successful. He wants peace, Colonel Peyton. So much so he's come here in person to show his good faith."

"If he wanted peace," the frigid tones burred back, "he'd be living on the reservation. You're the one the Crows call Lone Wolf," he said suddenly to Brett Baylor.

"I am. Though that has no importance in this matter."

"It does to me. Once a renegade, always a renegade. I've no proof you were on the train. For all of that, you might have been with the war party that pulled off the attack."

"A Crow warrior mixed in with the Sioux. Are you out of your mind?"

"I'll brook no impertinence from you, young man. Indians are Indians."

"Colonel," Rebecca began in a strained voice. "How long have you been on the frontier? Surely you know that the Sioux and Crow are mortal enemies. Mr. Baylor, Lone Wolf, has been my friend and associate for a number of years. It was he who helped me get away from the Oglala originally."

"Then why are you back here with them now?"

Rebecca paused a moment. "Because Iron Calf was my father. Granted, he was a war chief, but in his later years he chose the path of peace. His people still want to live peacefully with their white neighbors. Only not on the reservation. The

71

train was attacked as a means of drawing attention to the plight of the nonreservation Sioux. You will note that there were very few men killed on either side, only a few wounded. This has not yet come to a war."

"Oh, yes, it has. Whites have been killed, as you so minimally pointed out, Miss Caldwell. That is yet another violation of the treaty by the Sioux."

"What about the unprovoked murders of Oglala women, children, and old people by whites? By civilians, not the Army, colonel. That's been happening a lot lately. Isn't that also a violation of the treaty?"

"Treaties with Indians aren't binding on whites. You should know that, Miss Caldwell. This is our country now, to expand into by right. The Indians must give way. As to these alleged attacks on Oglala villages, we have only the word of some savages. That is to say, we have no proof at all."

Rebecca took a determined step forward, anger rising faster than she could control. "I can't believe your closed-mindedness," she challenged. "Women and children are being killed in cold blood. Doesn't that affect you in the least?"

"*Indian* women and children. Renegades. Hostiles off the reservation. What happens to them is of no importance whatsoever."

"Yes it is, goddamn you."

"Sergeant Major," Peyton called aloud. When the senior NCO opened the door, the colonel went on in a quiet, rapid voice. "My compliments to the provost, and will he have armed guards sent to escort these . . . ah, these people out of my office."

"Sir, yes, sir."

"I'll not be spoken to in that manner, Miss Caldwell," Peyton went on in quiet fury, "nor will I be lectured as to the status of disobedient savages under my jurisdiction. You've brought the captives back. For that you have the Army's gratitude. Turn them over and be on your way, before I have White Buffalo and this other heathen clapped in irons."

"You son of a . . ." Rebecca began. Lone Wolf took her by the right arm and gave a slight shake of his head.

"You have the power to do what you will," Lone Wolf acknowledged. "We're not in agreement, and we're not through just yet."

"What do you propose to do?" Peyton sneered.

Recovered slightly, Rebecca answered him. "We'll go to the territorial governor, if necessary. We'll write to Washington. Somehow this situation will be resolved in a fair and just manner. And, oh, by the way. You have a bit of a problem on your hands. Two of the children . . ." Reflecting on Peyton's attitude toward Indians and things Indian, Rebecca bit off her remark in midsentence.

"Two of the children what?"

"Nothing important, Colonel. Only that two of the captives tend to exaggerate a little. Likewise a Miss Hawthorne, whom I'm sure you will find shares your opinions quite a bit. I wish you the joy of them, Colonel. Now, good day."

"Just a minute, young woman!" Peyton thundered. "I'll decide when this interview is terminated."

"Oh? Why, goodness, Colonel, I thought you just had. You did send for the guard mount to remove us, didn't you?"

"Damn you, woman!" A long pause followed. "All right. Get out."

Once outside the headquarters, Lone Wolf spoke quietly to Rebecca. "You cut off mention of Tommy and Chad. Don't you think the colonel should know what he's up against?"

"To answer in order, you're damned right I did. And no, I don't think he need know about two *Oglala* boys who are getting out of here with us."

"They're white, Becky. And they should be returned to their parents."

"Granted. But not after Peyton gets done with them. If he saw them in breechcloths and moccasins, he'd probably have them strapped to a wagon wheel and beaten within an inch of their lives."

Lone Wolf produced a reluctant grin. "It wouldn't be impossible, I suppose. And when he *does* find out, because Sally Hawthorne will spare no effort to inform him, it's sure to make him furious."

"That's his problem, not ours. At least, for the time being. What we need to do now is gather *all* of our Oglala friends and head for Pierre. Like I said in there, we'll damn well see the territorial governor."

Chapter 8

Big blue eyes saucered on Rebecca Caldwell, Tommy Archer blurted out his excitement. "You mean you've changed . . . that we're gonna go . . ."

"*No, damnit,* speak only in Lakota," Rebecca hissed. "Don't respond to anything a soldier or anyone says in English. From now on you're Mahtociquala and you, Chad, are Cekpa Tanka. Follow Tipsila Ce's lead. Show lots of face; look straight ahead and don't talk. Then, when we're outside the fort, you boys chatter it up in Lakota."

She, Lone Wolf and Whirlwind hurried the boys away from the other captives. Fortunately Tipsila Ce had been there talking with Tommy and Chad and so the incident had attracted no particular attention from the soldiers lounging about. Several thought it odd that an Oglala boy should have hair so blond as Tommy's, but they heard the rapid fire exchange in the liquid gutturals of Lakota and figured that there had probably been a white trapper or gold prospector in the wood-pile somewhere.

Once clear of the big main gate, Tommy let out a whoop of exuberance. "We did it!" he shouted in Lakota. "We got away with it. I thought ol' Miss Hawthorne would bust her corset."

"We're gonna live with the Sayaota!" Chad sang in Lakota. "Say, what does Cekpa mean?"

"This," Tipsila Ce responded, placing a finger on the smooth knot of his navel.

"Big Bellybutton, huh?" Chad mused, slipping into English. "Oh, well, I guess it fits."

Dust and lumps of sod flew behind ten horses' hoofs, obscuring the dwindling facade of Camp Cullen. Anger still boiled in Rebecca's breast, barely beneath the surface. Lieutenant Colonel Peyton had been an ass. A simplistic idiot who saw all things in extremes of black and white. Something unknown to her had fed his typical white man's dislike of Indians into white-hot hatred. With the passing miles, her mood cooled.

First she had to make one thing absolutely clear. "I want you boys to understand this," she began when they slowed their animals to a walk to let them blow. "Your being with us is only a temporary thing. Once we're sure you are free of the tender loving care of Colonel Peyton, you're still going back to your parents. We'll make arrangements in Pierre."

"You can't!" Tommy cried in defiance. "Blokanumpa wants me for his brother. His father and mother want me, too. An' you told Miss Hawthorne I was already adopted," he added hopefully.

"That was only a convenient fiction, for Sally Hawthorne's sake. I realize they want you, but your parents would never condone such a thing."

"No! *Please* don't make me do that!" Tommy's sharp soprano knifed at Rebecca's heart.

To her surprise, she saw tears welling in the boy's eyes. His expression, mixed of hurt and despair, tugged at her long-buried maternal emotions. Tipsila Ce, equally stricken, looked at her as though betrayed. Chad had a rose-tinted pout on his full lips and his eyes were those of a trapped animal. The total effect made her want to hate herself. But she knew she was right. Both white boys had homes and families who loved and missed them. Right was right, and she could not turn away from it.

76

"No arguments and no appeals. We have to do what is right for you and for your families. There'll be no more talk of it."

That, she hoped, ended that.

"Hostiles ahead, sir," Corporal Wilson informed Lieutenant Larsen. "About three miles. Beyond that gap in the divide."

"Very well," Arnulf Larsen replied, returning the corporal's salute. "Is Granger keeping track of them?"

"Yes, sir. He sent me to let you know. There's about twenty warriors, all heavily armed. They're Sioux, right enough."

"Sergeant Thompkins."

"Sir!"

"See to the men's equipment and reloads. When we reach the top of that rise, I'll have them deployed into attack formation."

"Yes, sir. You heard the lieutenant," he growled to the men. "I want those cartridge pouches unbuckled, same for your holsters. Carbines loose in their scabbards. No smoking an' no loud noises. We're gonna go kick some Sioux ass."

"Forward at the canter . . . Ho-o-o!" Larsen commanded.

Over the previous five days, Larsen had carefully kept the patrol clear of White Buffalo's village. He had a strong suspicion that the hostiles had originated there, but harbored no desire to attempt a confrontation among all those Oglala braves. Orders might be one thing, but common sense frequently was another. Here, in an independent command, he had the option to exercise whichever one he felt inclined toward. Besides, he'd come to like the old man, respect him. When White Buffalo said he wanted peace, he believed him. With a sense of impending dread, he wondered what they would find the othe side of the rise.

It turned out to be a hunting party. In the interim between their discovery and Corporal Wilson's report, they had downed three fat buffalo and set about skinning them out. When the cavalry charged in among them, firing their carbines, the sentinels grabbed up their weapons and exchanged shots. Quickly the blood-splattered hunters joined in.

A wild melee ensued. The two lines clashed, and Lieutenant Larsen lost control over his men. They milled about, on horseback and afoot, gripped in individual combats with the Indians. The rippling volleys that had at first been fired degenerated into random shots. The grunts and screams of men were harsh to Larsen's ears. A blur of motion resolved into a warrior close on his right, a stone-headed war club swinging toward Larsen's head. Larsen raised his revolver and fired automatically, without need for conscious thought.

Through the fog of powder smoke, Lieutenant Larsen saw the Oglala fling himself away with a howl, one hand reaching for the red-spurting gouge the officer's bullet had put in the thick flesh at the juncture of his neck and shoulder. Then, ahead of him and distinctly, Larsen saw clear ground. Jamming the blunt knobs of his cavalry spurs into his horse's flanks, he plunged through to the far side of the battle. As best they could, his men followed him.

Instantly the Sioux retaliated. Howling, they flung themselves on their attackers. Furious at having been attacked for no seeming cause, they fought like wild beings. Here and there wounds streamed blood and they saw several of the blue-suits dripping scarlet. The soldiers rallied and broke off at a shouted command and the pealing notes of a bugle.

"Trumpeter, sound *Recall*."

Leading the way, Lieutenant Larsen galloped off a short distance, then turned back. He and the Oglala braves eyed each other with hostile intent. Sergeant Thompkins reported to him.

"Nobody down, sir. An' only three cut up some."

"Very well, Sergeant."

"We bloodied 'em a bit, sir."

"That we did. They're a hunting party, Sergeant. You can see that. They're not painted for war, so I've a feeling we got the wrong ones."

"Injuns is Injuns, as the colonel says, sir."

"Not this time. We've had a good general roughing up, which is something the Sioux appreciate. Before we make it worse, I think it would be wise to withdraw."

"Sir? Beggin' your pardon, sir, but do you mean we're to pull off without finishin' them?"

"Exactly, Sergeant."

Thompkins shrugged. "Yer in charge, sir. Whatever you say, sir."

Arnulf Larsen wished he had the Lakota words to explain to these unsuspecting hunters they had jumped. All the same, for better or worse, right or wrong, he'd made his decision, and he determined to stick by it.

Nightfall caught the determined group still on the trail, though a comfortable distance from Camp Cullen. Whirlwind and the three boys located a quiet, mossy spot in a creek and pulled enough fish from it to feed them all well. Along with some cornbread that Rebecca made and some wild onions, it provided quite a feast. Rebecca intended to slip away with Whirlwind later on and waited quietly while the camp drifted off into slumber. She rose then, taking her blankets, and started across the camp.

A whimper arrested her movement. More like the squeak of a frightened mouse or rabbit, the sound came again, and she located the source. The buffalo robe over Tommy's shoulders shook slightly and another plaintive mew came from there. Swiftly Rebecca knelt at Tommy's side. She placed a hand on his thin shoulder and he cringed away. Then he turned up a tear-stained face.

"What's the matter, Tommy," she asked quietly. "Why are you crying?"

"C-Cause you're gonna take me back. Please don't, Miss Rebecca. Oh, *please* don't. M-My dad's as yellow as an egg-suckin' dog. He don't stand up for himself, or for me, he don't stand up for nothin'. An' my mother is just awful to me. She hates me, told me lots of times she wished I'd never been born." Tommy gulped and began to sob wildly. Rebecca took him in her arms.

"There now, Tommy. Let it all come out. Surely she isn't so awful as you paint her."

"Sh-she is," he blubbered. "It's just an act when she's nicey-nice in front of other folks. She's mean, real mean. She beats me with a big ol' wooden paddle and says it's because she loves me. An' she's cut me with a knife, even burned me. Put my hand on the cookstove once because I wet my pants."

Hesitantly Tommy exposed his left hand, palm up. An ugly pucker of scar tissue covered a large part of it. He shivered and flung himself against Rebecca's breast.

"Sometime she's gonna kill me. She will when she learns what I did after we left the train. Please don't let her get her hands on me."

Deeply moved by the child's words and the sight of the ugly scar, iron formed in Rebecca's core. How could any parent treat a child like that? Her jaw firmed and she considered means of rectifying the situation. First, she had to be certain.

"What about your sister, Tommy? Does she treat her like that, too?"

Tommy's face grew serious, eyes big. "Oh, no. She'd never do that. She buys Bessie all sorts of things. Dolls, and shoes, and more clothes than she can ever wear. I've gotta make do with hand-me-downs from that church of hers. That's because Bessie's a *girl*. It's boys she hates."

"You said she had cut you, Tommy. I've never seen any scars on you. Show me where."

Hesitantly, though obviously from shame and humiliation rather than modesty, Tommy crawled from his covers and stood, turned away from Rebecca. He pulled off his loincloth and revealed a swatch of snowy white, in stark contrast to the rich brown his legs and back had become. Disgust and horror filled Rebecca as her eyes made out the ugly red welts of the knife scars.

"That's not all, either." Tommy turned slowly around.

Rebecca nearly gagged when she saw the slash mark on Tommy's partly distended penis. His explanation was the catalyst that solidly set her mind on a course of action.

"She did it one time when she was really mad. Said she hated me for being a boy. That all men were evil. She would cut off my peter and take away the sin from me."

"Oh, my God," Rebecca gulped out. "Tommy, put back your loincloth. And, Tommy, oh dear Tommy, you can be sure of one thing. You'll never, never see that woman again. You have a new home now. With the Oglala or with me, until we can see what your father would do to help you."

"He won't," Tommy replied tonelessly.

"Let's give him a chance. First, let me deal with your mother—the word sticks in my mouth when applied to a woman like that—then we'll find out what your dad wants."

Hope illuminated the small boy's face. "Would you? Would you really do that for me?"

"Yes, I will. And no matter how it comes out, no matter who you eventually go to live with, you'll never have to be afraid again. That, I promise you."

Transported, filled with trust, Tommy flung his arms around Rebecca's neck and hugged her with surprising strength. "Oh, I love you, Miss Rebecca. You're the most wonderful person in the world."

Chapter 9

Flame crackled around a fat log in the spacious walk-in fireplace. A whole steer had been roasted there last year to commemorate the completion of construction. Built entirely from native fieldstone, the imposing, three-story structure at the corner of Water Street and Custer in Pierre, Dakota Territory housed the Dakota Cattlemens' Association. The billiard tables in the game room—there were three of them—had been imported from New York City and boasted of "genuine Italian marble" bases under the green felt playing surface. "From the palaces of the Caesars," Alystaire Carmoody frequently bragged. Carmoody sat now in a deep wing-back leather chair before the fire.

Late fall's chill had already permeated the walls of this bastion of wealth and power. The crackling cottonwood billets helped to push it back. Gathered in the big room with Carmoody were five of the members, including Grover Ridgeway and Sam Bascomb. Carmoody's mood was sour.

"We've set policy in this room before, Sam," Carmoody replied to a question asked by the spare, dapper, white-haired Bascomb. "Lot's of times. And carried it out, too. We decided there would be no more than seven of us to carve up the territory for our cattle enterprise. We hired regulators to run off or exterminate the vermin who moved in to run a few hundred head, and those who came with plows to break the sod. This is *our* land. The damned Sioux have got to go. We agreed on that. The Army's on the edge. Grover and I saw to that a few days ago."

"You went to see that old fire-eater, Peyton," Sam acknowledged. "Did it do any good?"

"You bet," Carmoody responded with enthusiasm. "Only not enough and not soon enough. Peyton has patrols out, looking for the renegades who shot up the Frisco train. So what happens? The same damned day we're there, some feller and a young gal bring in the captives, along with a Sioux chief. They want to talk peace. Peyton has to listen to them. He'd get fried by department headquarters if he didn't. We heard about it at the stage stop last night. The thing is, if they manage to cool off Peyton, then we're in real trouble."

"So what do you propose, Alystaire?" Harry McCall grunted out.

Carmoody considered his prepared response carefully, weighed the strengths and limitations of each man in the room, before answering. "We've got to keep the Sioux stirred up. Get them boiling mad. Then the Army can't ignore what is going on."

"But, if our regulators are caught provoking the Sioux, we could be in big trouble," Sam Bascomb protested. "There's a lot of feeling back East. . . ."

Carmoody raised a hand to stop his friend. "Spare me all that. Ever since that poet—a *poet* for Christ's sake—published his milksop tale about the 'noble redman', every woebegone and sob-sister East of the Mississippi has been making hay by criticizing the Administration's 'Indian policy'. Well, I don't give a damn about them, or about their supposed influence. What I do care about is turning this territory into one big, open-range cattle operation, with us, gentlemen, *us* calling the shots. It's either that, or we'll soon be on our way to Kansas, with our tails between our legs, looking to homestead a quarter-section farm.

84

"I say we turn our range detectives loose. Let's give the regulators free rein to do whatever they think will drive the Oglala into a general uprising. Then, as I told Grover the other day, we can let the Army do our killing for us." Flinty eyes moved from one to another. "Grover, Sam, Ned, Harry, Will, what do you think? Are you with me?"

"Yeah."

"Yep."

"Count me in."

From chair to chair, agreement passed around the room. The fate of the free Sioux was sealed.

NO INJUNS, NIGGERS, DOGS, OR IRISH!

The bold black letters appeared on placards at many stores in Pierre and at every hotel. The atmosphere had changed considerably since Rebecca had last been in the territorial capital. She exchanged a troubled glance with Lone Wolf and they walked away from the last establishment. In a narrow byway they found quiet and privacy enough to converse.

"Looks like we'll be camping outside of town," Lone Wolf observed.

"Fine with me. *Civilization!*" Rebecca exclaimed acidly. "The more I see of it the more I think we'd be wise to go off and live with the Sayaota."

"All we have to do is put on our fancy duds and they'd welcome us with open arms," Lone Wolf mocked.

"We'll do that when we visit the governor tomorrow. As for now, I can do without these fine people's company."

Out in a grove of apple trees, on a small abandoned farm, the Oglala delegation had already set up a campsite. When Rebecca and Lone Wolf returned with supplies, they greeted their lack of welcome with blank-faced acceptance. They had expected no more. The three small boys in the party had gone off adventuring around the farm.

They had found piles of leaves and rotten fruit from the trees and had had a fight that left them fragrant with the odor of fermented apples. They had explored the barn before returning, shortly after Rebecca's arrival. Grinning, they stood with arms akimbo and made their report. Tommy, naturally, was the spokesman.

"We can sleep in the barn," he began.

"Or the house," Chad added, a bit wistfully Rebecca thought.

"It's nice under the trees, too," Tommy added.

"So we see . . . and smell. You three are bound for a scrubbing."

"There's a windmill that works," Tommy informed her. "And a wooden stock tank. That oughtta do."

Surprised at such a willing response, Rebecca studied Tommy and Chad gravely. "I've never seen eleven- and twelve-year-old boys so anxious to take a bath."

A wry grin split Tommy's face. "Beaver's been tellin' us that the Oglala take a bath every day. Sometimes more than that." He shrugged eloquently. "I guess we've gotta get used to it."

"Off with you then, and get that windmill primed and pumping."

Quickly, she and Lone Wolf informed Ptasan Okiye and the others of what they had learned in town. The governor was in residence, and they had made a contact who could gain them access to set an appointment. It would be at least two days before they could expect to hold a meeting. Talk of Indian troubles could be heard everywhere, and the local newspaper made big of supposed raids by the Sioux. Predictably, no mention was made of white raiders attacking the Oglala villages.

"Will they send soldiers to bind us when we ride into town?" White Buffalo Helps Him inquired.

"No. We'll make arrangements in advance. Maybe the governor will want to meet with us away from the pressures of the capitol and town."

"Hello the camp," came a hail from the farm lane.

"Hello," Lone Wolf echoed back. "Ride on in."

"Sure enough, young feller. An' I know . . . keep my hands in sight."

A horse snorted and its hoofs clopped on the hard dirt of the lane. In a moment a squat figure in slouch hat and rumpled clothing came into view. He rode with a Winchester across the saddlehorn. Orange-red hair made a fringe around his ears. He drew nearer and his pale blue eyes twinkled like the sunlight off the star on his corduroy coat.

"Philo Bates, dep'ty U.S. marshal," he announced.

"I'm, ah, Brett Baylor," Lone Wolf told him. "This is Rebecca Caldwell and, . . ."

"I know this old rapscallion. *How-cola, Ptasan Okiye.*"

"*How-cola,* Phi-lobates," White Buffalo Helps Him responded gravely, a fleeting smile adding creases to his lined face.

"You've come a long way," Bates went on in Lakota.

"I come in peace, Phi-lobates."

"Is it your bucks kicking up a fuss west of here?"

"Some of the young men. We come to talk peace with the Little White Father."

"The governor's not gonna be too pleased about that," Bates said in English.

"Why is that?" Rebecca injected.

"There was captives taken from a Frisco train."

"We know about that. Mr. Baylor and I were on board. We brought the captives back and left them at Camp Cullen."

Loud, joyful squeals and noisy splashing came from the direction of the barn. Bates looked that way and caught a flash of small, bare, brown bottom over the top of the stock tank. His shaggy eyebrows elevated in an unspoken question.

"The Šayota brought along some children to show their peaceful intent. They'd become friends with a number of the captive boys."

"That's odd. Usual is that captives are treated a bit worse

87

than Sioux dogs—an' that's sayin' a mouthful.''

"We, ah, that is, White Buffalo Helps Him convinced the war party to make the captives into guests. No one was harmed at all.''

"Ow! Hey, don't pinch my butt," Chad Bennett yelled distinctly in English.

So much for that, Rebecca thought as Bates gave her a long, thoughtful stare. He swung from the saddle and started off in the direction of the barn.

"I think I'd like to get a look at these Oglala kids you mentioned.''

"Wait, Marshal. If you'd let me explain first, I think it would make a considerable difference.''

"*That* might take a passel of 'explainin'.'"

Swiftly, not holding back a single terrible detail of Tommy's wretched home life, Rebecca outlined the boy's situation. Whirlwind acknowledged the truth of it when she told of Tommy's impending adoption by the Oglala. She concluded with what she hoped would be a beneficial solution.

"So we felt it better for Tommy to stay with us until his father could be contacted and determine what could be done for the boy.''

"Parents own a kid," the marshal said with finality. "Just like a horse or a dog. It's the law. Can't go separatin' 'em from their folks without an order from the court. Especially to give a boy away to the Sioux.''

"My uncles gave me away to the Sioux when I was fourteen,'' Rebecca replied quietly.

Bates squinted at her. "T'hell you say. Ah, pardon me, ma'am. But I find it highly unusual.''

"Think, marshal. Doesn't the name Caldwell mean anything to you?''

"Hummm. There was an Ezekiel and a Virgil Caldwell, penny-ante owlhoots a few years back. Seems as how I heard about Virgil bein' killed by some slip of a girl, durin' a stampede.''

"That's right, Marshal. I did for him. Right between the eyes. He was my uncle, so's Ezekiel. Though chances are Ezekiel will be dead before spring."

"An' this boy's momma actually burnt his hand because she was mad at him?"

"That's what he said, and I believe him. He's a scared, confused little boy, Marshal. It would be a crime to return him to someone like that. Tommy doesn't want to live with his father, but if Mr. Archer realized the evil she's done and put his wife aside, I think he could find himself and be man enough to raise the boy properly."

"An' that's your whole interest in the matter?"

"Honestly, Marshal."

His keen blue eyes made Rebecca feel as though they bored holes through her. "Well, you've lived among the savages. Don't seem to have harmed you any. Which bunch was it, anyway?"

"My father, Iron Calf, was war chief of the Red Top Lodges before he died."

"Well, I'll be double damned. Small world, ain't it? Now, I don't hold any particular strong case for the Oglala, mind. But I've heard, and even observed from time to time, that they don't beat on their youngin's the way us white folk do. I've never been married, got no kids I know of. Onliest thing, as a lawman most of my adult years, I've come to find that hardcases gen'rally come from kids whose folks whaled the tar outta 'em. Bein' tough became a way to survive."

"Harsh punishment doesn't affect everyone that way, marshal, but in some cases, I think you might have a point," Rebecca agreed, hope flickering alive again. "In which case, Marshal Bates, you might go over there and see only Small Bear of the Šayota Oglala swimming with his friends, or you might yank a towheaded white boy out of the water by his ear, and take away to his mother's loving care the next Jesse James."

"You sure know how to put a man betwixt a rock an' a

89

. . . oh, gosh-dang it, woman, I'll go along with you. At least for the time bein'."

"Thank you, Marshal Bates."

Bates's eyes narrowed. "You said you come to see the governor. My guess is it ain't just about that train shoot-up."

Rebecca and Lone Wolf explained about the raids by white men on isolated groups of the Red Top Lodge Oglala. Rebecca made the point that primarily women and children were being killed. Bates listened intently, accepted a cup of coffee, and sipped on it while the events unfolded. At last he smacked his lips, brushed away the now-soggy ends of his flowing mustache, and bit off a corner from his plug of Horseshoe.

"Sounds to me like this-here Dakota Cattlemen's Association. They've been hirin' ever' saddle tramp and two-bit gunhawk that come driftin' into the territory. They're a power with the elected officials, more's a pity. Though there's only seven of 'em in the inner circle, they swing a mighty big club.

"There's strong reason to suspect that they, an' their regulators, are behind the sudden deaths of a number of small ranchers and farmers. I ain't got the evidence of it, but I keep my eye on them regulators best I can. I strongly suspect the way it works is that the members are safe enough from rustlers, but anyone else had better chain his cows to trees or lose them to sticky-loopers among these self-same 'Range Detectives.' As to how you say the Sioux have been treated of late, it's shameful. But I'm whipsawed between the marshal's office far off in Washington on one side, an' the Army and Cattlemen's Association on the other. An' none of them have any hanker to do right by the Injuns."

"If I understand you correctly, Marshal Bates, were you to get the right sort of evidence, you'd fall on the Cattlemen's Association and their regulators?"

"Like stink on a skunk, Miss Rebecca."

"Then why not throw in with us? If we get what we want, you'll have all the evidence you need."

Lips pursed, eyes atwinkle, Bates considered the proposition

90

a moment. "Now, that has a ring to it. I'll join up, an' gladly. Ah, how are you figgerin' to get ol' White Buffalo here in to see the governor?"

"We made a contact in town. A man named Winstead Oliver."

"Ummmm. Doubt you'll get far there. He hangs around the recess lobby of the legislature and tries to buttonhole members to see things go the way his interests want. If he don't have lots of money backin' his play, ain't likely he can get results. Bribes on this level don't go cheap."

"What can we do, then?"

A fleeting suggestion of amusement slid over Philo Bates's face and he winked slowly. "You might leave that up to me. Bein' a United States marshal gives me a little more clout."

Chapter 10

It began far off in the velvet black of their second night in the abandoned orchard. A faint, sibilant exhalation that grew nearer and more insistent awakened Rebecca Caldwell. A sudden, sharp drop in temperature gave scant warning before the front swept on them. Like the persistent hissing of leaking steam, or a million mice racing through the crisp brown grass, frozen rain fell in sheets across the prairie.

The heavy sleet coated tree limbs and glazed the sides and roofs of buildings. In the barn the horses nickered uneasily. Whirlwind stirred, grunted, and raised up on one elbow.

"What is it?"

"Sleet. We're in an ice storm."

Rebecca and Whirlwind had been apart from the others, sharing the thrills of love through the night. She swiftly pulled on her clothing and went to rouse the others.

"Get up," she said urgently. "Ice storm. Go into the buildings. Hurry," she repeated to the slumber-drugged forms she encountered around the empty farm. At last, all had been accounted for except Chad Bennett.

"Where's Chad?" Rebecca asked Tommy Archer.

"Oh, he's already inside," Tommy answered disdainfully. "He likes it better in the house."

Despite the rapidly deteriorating weather, this revelation

struck a note in Rebecca's memory. Of all those in their party, it had been Chad who had observed that they could sleep in the house. His voice had sounded wistful at the time. Perhaps playing Indian was beginning to wear a bit? If so, that was one less problem to solve. Rebecca left the others to make their own accommodations and headed for the house.

She found Chad in one of the bedrooms, curled up on a sagging bedstead. He whimpered when she touched him, then came groggily awake. "I . . . what's wrong, Miss Rebecca?"

"Nothing, Chad. There's an ice storm. Everyone's moving inside. You, ah, seem to like it here," she probed.

Slowly Chad nodded. "I . . . do. I, ah, guess I kinda want to go home."

"Just a little bit? Like you said?"

Chad hung his head, his rounded, little-boy chin resting on his bare chest. "N-no. I-I miss my Dad awful. A-a-and my Mom. I-it's not like with Tommy. I *love* my folks an' my brother and sister. This—this has b-been fun an' all, but . . ."

"Chad, we're finally going to see the governor tomorrow. Would you like to come into town with us and return to being a white boy?"

Chad bloomed with awakened hope. Eyes wide with eagerness, he placed a trusting hand on Rebecca's shoulder. "D'you mean I can? There wouldn't be . . . ? I mean, nobody's gonna . . . ? P-please, look the other way. I want to put on my loincloth and sit up so we can talk."

Rebecca wrinkled her brow thoughtfully as she turned away, hearing the rustling sounds behind her. "Has that bothered you, Chad?"

"Y-yes," he admitted in a small voice. Then, "It's all right now, you can turn around."

Rebecca faced the boy now, who sat cross-legged in the dumpy old bed. His eyes sparkled. He shivered in the chill draft from the broken window and covered himself with a heavy buffalo sleeping robe. Rebecca reached out and stroked his carroty hair.

"Chad, among the Indians there has never been the strong sense of shame about the human body that whites have. They wear clothes for comfort, convenience, modesty on the part of women, and to look nice. You've spent all of your life learning the white way. I'm not surprised that you feel a little uncomfortable. I can't say that the white way is right, or even superior to the Indian, considering some of the terrible things that have been done in the name of morality. Yet, it's your way and I respect your right to follow it. No one's holding you against your will. If you want to go home, you may. Then, if sometime, just for a while, you want to play Indian again, you may."

Relief sagged Chad's shoulders and he drew a deep, contented sigh from far down in his chest. "You *do* understand. I was afraid you wouldn't. Y'see, where I live, things are such that us boys have to wear our summer longjohns when we go swimming. Our folks would skin us alive if we didn't. We can't even go without a shirt on a hot day. Brown skin is considered sinful." The corners of Chad's mouth turned down and a momentary pout puckered his full lips. "I don't like it always, but . . . it's the way we are."

"And you'd rather go back to it." Rebecca made it a statement, not a question.

Chad nodded, a bit hesitantly, though gaining a positive strength. "Will you . . ." he began hesitantly. "Will you tell Tommy and Tipsi?"

"No," Rebecca answered him. "That's up to you to do. Particularly if you think that someday you might like to come visit. Now, goodnight. Sleep tight through this storm and we'll go into town tomorrow."

Creaks and groans came from the trees as morning sunlight began to stir up a breeze. Every trunk, branch, twig, and the few remaining leaves had been uniformly coated with a thick accumulation of ice. Here and there, sharp reports, like rifle shots, sounded when movement and weight combined to break off a limb. Even the buildings glistened in the weak sunshine, which promised no warmth.

Great puffs of vapor formed at everyone's mouth and nose, and the horses snorted, blowing clouds from their ice-tinged nostrils. Tipsila Ce had shared his winter clothing with Tommy Archer. Chad Bennett had dressed in his white boy's garb and shivered inside a buffalo robe. Tommy cast Chad a pleading glance.

"Sure you won't stay?"

"Un-huh. I—I'm sorry, Tommy, uh, Mahtociqala. I just . . . wanna to home."

"Okay," Tommy said lightly, using an expression recently becoming popular among the younger people in "civilization."

The term came from a certain inspector for the Union Army who had branded his initials, O.K., on barrels and hogsheads of flour, pork, and beef sent to the troops in the field. The mark indicated that the product met required standards. To the long-suffering soldiers at the battlefronts, the initials had become a guarantee against their normal rations of weevily flour, mouldy hardtack, rotten meat, and short counts on supplies. Whoever the anonymous O.K. happened to be, he had been one of the few honest inspectors on the Union side. Though not destined to come out of the war a rich man, his initials became a valued and respected seal of approval and later a universal American symbol of acceptance and agreement.

"Goo-bye," Tipisla Ce said in his severely limited English vocabulary.

"I'm gonna miss you, Chad," Tommy added throatily.

"I—I'll miss you guys, too."

"Time to leave," Rebecca interrupted, breaking up this tender moment before unmanly tears overflowed and embarrassed all of the boys.

They reached Pierre at the bustly hour of nine o'clock, when all the stores began to open for business. Despite the tingling cold, men and women flocked the boardwalks. Wagons, drays and carts filled the streets. Rebecca, Lone Wolf, Ptasan Okiye, and Whirlwind threaded their way through the sprawling crowd. Chad Bennett clung close beside the white squaw, his eyes alight with joy and eagerness. The trip had been timed to allow for a visit to the telegraph office first.

There, Chad gave the telegrapher's clerk his name and those of his parents, also where to wire in Nebraska. Rebecca dictated the text.

"Mr. Harlan Bennett, Waverly, Nebraska. Your son Chadwick is alive and well. He awaits reunion with you in Pierre, Dakota Territory. Please wire Rebecca Caldwell with information regarding your arrival here."

"Prob'ly be two, three hours," the telegraph operator said over his shoulder. "Come back then."

Far from what Rebecca had expected, after the opulence of Sacramento, the executive offices of Dakota Territory turned out to look exactly like what they had been; a slightly seedy, rundown hotel. An officious majordomo escorted them past ranks of secretaries, up two flights of stairs to a large suite on the third floor. There, in the outer room, another prissy young man kept them waiting for nearly half an hour before announcing that the governor would see them.

"How do you do," the governor said somewhat icily after the introductions. "I have to admit to not fully grasping the protocol of this visit. Am I to understand that White Buffalo speaks for all his people?"

"In this instance, yes," Rebecca answered. "Oh, ah, with your leave, governor, I'll act as translator."

"Quite all right, young lady. Somehow your name is familiar to me. Would you mind enlightening me?"

"Not at all. Do you recall an outlaw gang led by a man named Bitter Creek Jake Tulley?" At the governor's nod, Rebecca went on. "Then you'll remember when they were driven out of the territory. Two members of that gang, Ezekiel and Virgil Caldwell, were uncles of mine." Quickly Rebecca sketched out the details of her pursuit of the gang.

"An admirable goal, Miss Caldwell, I must admit," the governor declared at the end of her recitation. "Though one that few would expect a woman to undertake. Have you been successful in bringing the outlaws to justice?"

Rebecca favored him with a smile. "Only Roger Styles and Ezekiel Caldwell remain. Roger is in Mexico. Uncle Ezekiel is snowbound in the Sierra Nevada mountains."

For a brief moment the color drained from the governor's face. "My word. We were never notified of their apprehension or trial. Why was that?"

"Most of them never went to trial," Rebecca told him calmly. "Except before their Maker."

"Oh . . . ah . . . my. What has this to do with you bringing a hostile Sioux chief to my office?"

"Nothing. Except that after we left Ezekiel Caldwell trapped in Donner Pass, we made arrangements to return to Dakota Territory. We were on the Frisco train that some hotheads attacked a little over a week ago. In fact, the youngster waiting outside with Tatekohom'ni is the last of the captives to be returned. The others were left at Camp Cullen."

"So I've been informed. What, precisely, is your function?"

"I've been asked to act as a peace emissary between the Šayaota Oglala—whom you call the Red Top Lodge band—and your office. Ptasan Okiye and his people want to live in peace. They use only a small bit of the land, and wish to be allowed to continue to do so."

"I can appreciate that. This country has been theirs for centuries. Change is always hard to adapt to."

"It's more than that, governor. Lately, white men have been attacking smaller encampments of the Red Top Lodge band. They kill women and children and burn the lodges. When White Buffalo Helps Him appealed to the Army, he was told that nothing could be done. That if they did anything to protect themselves, they would be punished."

"I see. And I sympathize. However, policy dictates that the

98

Sioux be placed on reservations. Were they to do as they are supposed to, then protection could be afforded them."

"But that's in complete violation of the treaty, governor," Rebecca pressed. "This land was promised to the Sioux forever. What happened to that?"

"The cowardly massacre of General Custer and his men broke all of the treaties. The Sioux must learn to do as they are told or suffer the consequences."

"Then, you can do nothing?"

"I *will* do nothing. You really haven't anything to discuss or arbitrate. This land is white man's land now. The Sioux must give way. It's as simple as that. As to the white boy you mentioned, it is my duty to place him under the protection of the territorial government and take custody until his parents can be notified."

"He would rather stay with us."

A condescending smile formed on the governor's lips and he spoke with acid insincerity. "Your concern for the youngster's welfare is admirable and duly noted. However, no decent person, young or old, would wish to remain in the clutches of hostile Indians. Please surrender him to my secretary on your way out. This interview is terminated."

"I'm sorry, governor, that simply won't do."

"You're defying *me*?"

"In the matter of Chad Bennett, yes. Chad knows us and trusts us. A telegram has already been sent to his parents. We'll have an answer within another two hours. Until then, I feel he'll be better off in our company than among strangers. Particularly that prissy specimen you have outside your office."

Scowling, the governor demanded in a thunderous tone, "Explain yourself, young lady."

Her own anger fired by the governor's hypocrisy, Rebecca let her temper make her reply. "So far, Chad has been un-harmed. I have no intention of leaving him in the custody of someone who would probably have the boy's bung hole reamed out before the sun set. Good day, governor."

"Weren't you a little hard on him?" Lone Wolf asked some ten minutes later as the small group walked along the main avenue of Pierre.

"Do you mean the governor or that sissy in the striped pants and wing collar?"

"The governor, of course," Lone Wolf replied through a chuckle. "Maybe he doesn't know what he has for a secretary."

"You sensed it, too?"

"'*My-y-y*, what a handsome young man we have here,'" Lone Wolf mimicked in a falsetto. "He was all but scooping up Chad and eating him with a spoon."

"He never took his eyes off me. It made me feel all crawly."

"You've good instincts, Chad," Rebecca complimented him. "Let's find some place to eat. Without the governor's help, there's little we can do here. We'll wait for the reply to our telegram, then go back to the others."

"The Little White Father speaks falsely," White Buffalo Helps Him injected.

"That he does," Rebecca agreed, thinking of the governor's cynical rebuke.

When the telegram message arrived near mid afternoon, the response left Rebecca in somewhat of a quandary. "*Pleased to learn of Chadwick's health and condition,*" it read. "*Presently unable to afford expensive journey round-trip to Pierre. Give Chadwick our best. Please put him on train or stagecoach for Waverly at earliest convenience. Be sure he has money for meals. Harlan Bennett.*"

"Not even a thank you," Rebecca remarked in a sour tone.

Chad had been eagerly reading the telegram over Rebecca's shoulder as she sat on a bench outside the Western Union office. Now his smooth brow wrinkled and his mouth turned downward, the sure sign of an emotionally hurt child about to cry.

"I-I guess they don't want me as much as I want them," he suggested in a quavery voice.

Rebecca drew Chad around the bench and took him in her arms. "That can't be so, Chad."

"They don't l-l-love me," he all but wailed.

"Now, now, don't cry, my little dear. It'll all work out. I . . . have an idea."

"You do?" Hope flared again for Chad.

"Yes. We'll send another telegram and see if that doesn't stir things up a bit."

Inside she dictated crisply, while the clerk noted it down with a gray slate pencil. "Harlan Bennett, Waverly, Nebraska. Mr. Bennett. Since we are not a lending institution, nor inclined to send a child cross-country unescorted, Chadwick's departure for Waverly will be delayed indefinitely. You may come for him at your convenience. He is to be found among the Red Top Lodge band of the Oglala Sioux. There he will be among friends and loved ones who care for him and cherish his presence. Sign that Rebecca Caldwell."

Chad hopped up and down in agitation. "That'll get 'em sweatin'," he predicted.

True enough. Half an hour before sundown, a boy on a bicycle brought the reply in a yellow pulp envelope. *"Will be on morning train from Omaha. Harlan Bennett."*

Chapter 11

For a reunion, the Bennett family one was suitably tearful. Particularly so since Chad had had the opportunity to dwell overnight on his parents' initial reaction. Their apparent indifference over his welfare hurt the child deeply. Emotionally younger that Tipsila Ce, he lacked the maturity of the Oglala boy or the hard shell of an abused youngster like Tommy. Consequently, when his folks effusively made much over him on the railroad platform in Pierre, under the hard, watchful eyes of Rebecca Caldwell and Lone Wolf, Chad Bennett began to have doubts about his decision to return to parental care.

Accordingly, he made a wet and forlorn farewell to his new friends before they rode away to join the Šayaota escort for the return trip to White Buffalo Helps Him's village. Rebecca had taken silent, angry note of the pointed, excessive repugnance shown by Mrs. Bennett toward Tipsi and Tommy, both of whom wore warm Oglala winter clothing. It gave the young white squaw pause to wonder if Tommy's choice might not be the right one. Not to belabor the point, she said nothing as the small band started out toward Camp Cullen.

"I want to give the Army one more try," Rebecca expounded while they walked their horses a good ten miles from Pierre.

"What do you expect to gain from a man like Peyton?" Lone

Wolf asked.

"Not much, granted," Rebecca admitted. "His agreement to act against troublemaking whites in the event we brought him proof would satisfy me right now."

"You might be asking too much even with that."

"We'll see," Rebecca responded philisophically. "At least we have to try."

They arrived at Camp Cullen the next day, during the midday mess call. Troopers filled the eating halls and the parade ground lay deserted as they walked their mounts across the hard-packed expanse to the headquarters building. There they dismounted, and Rebecca entered with Lone Wolf at her side. Sergeant Major Roach greeted them.

"I'm sorry, miss. Colonel Peyton won't be able to receive you until after noon chow. If you'll be so kind as to wait, I'll inform him you are here."

"Thank you, Sergeant Major," Rebecca replied, careful to get the noncom's rank correct.

Fortunately, the sun held little warmth. The little delegation was compelled to wait on the open parade while the post went about dining. Stomachs growled at the odor of food wafting by them from the mess halls. A few troopers, finished with their meal, eyed them curiously and ambled away to smoke or grab a few moments' nap before returning to duty. At ten minutes past one, Lt. Col. Bryce Peyton stepped through the door of headquarters and stood on the roofed porch, hands on hips.

"I see you're back. I hope, for your sakes, it's to surrender these renegades to us for proper punishment."

"What do you mean?" Rebecca demanded.

"While this jackal came here to treacherously whine for peace, a war party he had dispatched attacked one of my patrols. Fortunately none of the troopers lost their lives, though several were wounded. Otherwise, I'd hang you all."

"I don't believe this," Rebecca began indignantly. "There were no war parties, I'll swear to that. Only some peaceful hunters out to make meat for the village."

Peyton cocked his head to one side and peered icily at Rebecca as though she had become some odd specimen of a heretofore unknown species. His lips curled contemptuously and he puffed like a toad before responding.

"My official report has been filed with Department Headquarters. Are you questioning its veracity?"

"Yes. Its, or rather, yours," Rebecca told him pointedly. "Having been in Ptasan Okiye's village, and speaking the language, I'm in a better position than you to know whether or not raiding parties had been sent out. I'm telling you now, *there were none.*"

"And I'm expected to take your word over that of an officer of my command? I have neither the time nor the inclination to stand here and debate the matter with you, young lady. If you and this, ah, *gentleman* wish to ride out of here unaccosted, I suggest you do so at once. I've already sent for troops to arrest these murderers. As for the boy, Tommy Archer, I'm taking custody of him immediately."

A glance over her shoulder showed Rebecca two squads of soldiers trotting across the parade ground, Springfields at the ready, bayonets fixed. She turned abruptly and swung into the saddle.

"Mount up. Ride like the wind," Rebecca commanded rapidly in Lakota.

"Sergeant Reinike, arrest these people!" Colonel Peyton bellowed. "All of them."

"Ride Tommy," Rebecca yelled, lashing the hindquarters of his pony with her quirt.

Milling in confusion at first, the Oglala braves, their chief, and the rest swung their mounts one way, then the other, before kicking heels into flanks and lining out toward the main gate. In a knifing moment of horror, Rebecca saw White Buffalo Helps Him hesitate, then turn back to the infuriated colonel.

"I come in peace. I have the medal of the White Father in Washington."

105

Ptasan Okiye raised the large medallion high to emphasize his poor English. "I come talk peace."

"Don't let a one get away!" Peyton screamed in a frenzy of hatred. "Open fire, men, open fire!"

Two .45-70 slugs smashed into Ptasan Okiye's back a moment later. Another pierced his intestines from side to side, while a fourth shattered his jaw at the right hinge. Blood flew in all directions. Tispila Ce howled in anguish at seeing his grandfather so foully murdered and raced his pony toward the nearest soldier, wielding his small rabbit bow.

Before he could loose an arrow, the trooper gleefully drove his bayonet through Tipsila Ce's left side, front to rear, and lifted the boy off his horse. Close by, Whirlwind and Tommy Archer saw the awful blow struck and swung toward the child, who writhed on the ground, hands covering the wound.

"You ba-a-a-astard!" Tommy shouted as he rode down the soldier who had wounded his friend.

Hard hoofs pounded the hapless assassin's chest and Tommy swung his leg over to drop to the ground. Whirlwind slammed the chest of his horse into another cavalryman who was about to shoot Tommy and smashed at his face with a large stone war club.

Bloodied and unconscious, the trooper fell away as Tommy slid from his pony and ran to Tipsila Ce. The single braided hair rein looped around his wrist, Sioux style, Tommy drew his mount to him, and with Whirlwind's help, lifted the wounded boy to the pony's back before swinging atop the prancing animal. Then he sped away in a whirl of dust.

Rebecca and Lone Wolf, who acted as rear guard, methodically fired their six-guns. They carefully aimed high to avoid killing any of the soldiers, yet close enough to cause them to duck. When they reached the still open gate, they paused once more. Colonel Peyton fired at them while he bellowed for A Company to saddle up and pursue.

"I want to kill that son of a bitch, so help me I do," Rebecca ground out.

"Some other time," Lone Wolf told her, his own fighting spirit aroused. "Now we've got to get away from here fast."

"And do something about Tipsi."

"What's the meaning of this?" Bryce Peyton demanded ten minutes later. "Why aren't your men saddled up and in pursuit of those renegades?"

"Because I didn't order them to do so," Lieutenant Arnulf Larsen replied steadily.

"That much is obvious, Mr. Larsen," Peyton's steely voice replied. "May I inquire as to the reason for this dereliction?"

"I'm no longer in command of A Company, Colonel Peyton."

"What do you mean?"

"I've resigned. I heard your conversation with the people you are now calling renegades. You totally changed my initial report on the skirmish with Oglala hunters and wrote a distorted false report to headquarters. I know, because I checked in the orderly room. The copy is there for anyone to see, also my own written notes. You then shot down—murdered—a man who was not resisting, who in fact called for peace. Then you allowed a small boy to be bayoneted. I have resigned because I can't remain under your command and file a complaint against you at department headquarters."

"There'll be no such complaint," Peyton snarled. "You'll file nothing and there will not be any contradictory notes. These supposed people, this man and child you refer to are Sioux Indians, Lieutenant. *Vermin!* The ones responsible for the murder of George Custer and the Seventh. The old one was a treacherous fool. The young one on the verge of being a warrior. Killing the one prevented more trouble in the present. The brat dying before he could breed means there'll be a dozen or so less warriors to face in the future. You *will* rewrite your notes to conform to my report and you *will* lead this expedition to capture the renegades."

107

"No, sir!"

Peyton recoiled as though he had been slapped. "Provost Marshal! Arrest this officer and place him in confinement in the guardhouse."

Graying, pot-bellied Captain Duncan Stanley came forward, giving a slight shake of his head in regret. "Come along, Lieutenant."

"My court martial board will hear all about this," Arnulf Larsen threatened.

He immediately regretted his rash declaration when he saw the light of madness in Bryce Peyton's eyes. It sent a shiver up Larsen's spine.

"Only if you live long enough to go to trial," Peyton said in a hollow tone.

Long shadows crossed the ground, and the last trills of the meadowlarks had stilled. Off to the east, toward distant Camp Cullen, an owl hooted. Tipsila Ce lay whimpering in pain, while Whirlwind and Big Nose fashioned a travois to ease the lad's strain on their journey. They would have to travel at night, to keep out of sight of the soldiers who would surely pursue them. That would make for rougher going. Rebecca Caldwell had dressed the wound, cleaning it with water, then packing the hole with a medicinal poultice of fresh herbs. Tipsila Ce had been lucky, she declared.

The wicked steel had sliced through his body at a point where little chance existed for internal damage. It would be slow to heal and the danger of infection remained. She would have preferred for a qualified doctor to examine him, yet she knew of no way to do that.

"You witnessed what happened," she said tightly to U.S. Marshal Philo Bates.

"Yes. The soldiers fired first, and except for the one that tried to gut the li'l nipper and the other who nearly shot young, ah, Small Bear, not a one of them got harmed. Though I can't

108

hold with taking up arms against the military authority."

"Self-defense," Rebecca returned. "Peyton is insane. You must know that."

"Yes. Considerin' I was lookin' down the muzzles of more'n one Springfield, with no never-you-mind about my bein' a United States marshal, I reckon there ain't a better word to describe him."

"I ain't never goin' back to the whites," Tommy Archer declared in his misery. "Someday I'm comin' back. Someday I'm gonna kill that shit-heel with the silver stars on his shoulders."

"Not stars," Philo Bates corrected automatically. "Oak leaves. Silver oak leaves. He's a lieutenant colonel."

"Oh . . . okay, oak leaves," Tommy responded absently. "Is Tipsi gonna die, Miss Rebecca?"

"No, Tommy. At least, I don't think so."

"He's awful hurt. An' so pale."

"Tipsi has lost a lot of blood. And a wound like that causes severe shock. We'll know more tomorrow."

"I—I'm gonna pray for him tonight. Is that all right? It'll just be to Jesus, but I hope the Great Spirit hears. I don't know how to pray to Him."

Rebecca's throat tightened and she reached out to ruffle the serious, big-eyed boy's straw-blond hair. "He'll understand you, Small Bear. Believe me."

With a festive ring, the rims of crystal champagne glasses touched around the room. Gentlemen in tailcoats, ladies in their most elegant attire, they filled the huge dining room of Grover Ridgeway's spacious ranch house. A hind quarter of prime beef turned on a spit over a bed of oak and hickory coals, small blue flames licking upward as rendered fat dripped from the meat. In one corner four men in formal evening wear sawed industriously on violin, viola, cello and pianoforte, grinding out the works of Mozart to an unappreciative audience.

Although the party was staged in these remote surroundings, the actual hosts were Alystaire Carmoody and Branch Delano.

"You've had remarkable success, Branch," Carmoody said expansively as he accepted another glass of the effervescent wine.

"I can almost see my name on the land claim now," Delano responded. "We're doing so well I think we ought to step up our raids on the damned Sioux."

"I thought we'd agreed not to discuss this tonight," Grover Ridgeway injected acidly.

"Oh, come on, Grover," Carmoody cajoled, one arm around his fellow conspirator. "How can you have a party without talking about the reason for it?"

"Half of the people here, the ladies at least, haven't the slightest idea what or why we're celebrating. To them it's a chance to show off their finery and gossip with friends. They'd be horrified if they knew."

"I'm not so shertain of that," Carmoody returned. He'd consumed a bit more than his share of the champagne and showed the effects in slightly slurred speech.

"Right. Loosen up, Grover. We've got no more of those heathen bastards left except ol' White Buffalo an' his band."

"You're talking about forty to fifty warriors, Branch," Ridgeway cautioned. "That's a few more than I'm anxious to take on."

Carmoody waved a hand in negligent dismissal. "We'll let the Army take care of them, like I said. Look on the bright side. Consider all the money we're gonna make. An' how good it will be not to have a single red savage within three hundred miles. It'll be ours, Grover, all ours."

"Your friend Peyton seems determined to kill every Indian from here to the Pacific. I'm not all that sure we want to be connected with a fanatic."

"Wash wha' you say about ol' Bryce, Grove. He's good people. You can believe that. He had a son, right bright lad at that. His hope for the future, you might say. He was a young

110

lieutenant in the cavalry. Got himself killed back at the Washita, ridin' with Custer against the Cheyenne. Ol' Georgie grieved over it 'bout as much as Bryce. Together they took an oath to make ever' redskin pay for the boy's death. Other'n that, he's a God-fearin', Christian gentleman.

"Why, back during the War of the Se-cession, he even gave his troops an order to capture all the Rebs they could, not to kill 'em. It's all gonna work out, Grover. You'll see. We can trust Bryce Peyton to do just exactly what's needed."

Chapter 12

Faded now, the stars hung against a curtain washed to a gray-dusted charcoal as the pearly ribbon of false dawn momentarily brightened the eastern horizon. Frost covered sagebrush and gamma grass, blurred the outlines of scattered tree limbs. A numbing cold made movements stiff and uncoordinated. The end of the second night's flight from Camp Cullen held out a single promise.

Not long after daylight, they should be within sight of the lodges of the Šayaota Oglala. Tipsila Ce slept restlessly on his travois, fevered, drifting in and out of consciousness. For the last two hours, Rebecca had ordered Tommy Archer bundled in with the wounded child to provide greater warmth. For a while the boys had snuggled together and slept peacefully. Now Tipsila Ce roused and cried out in pain.

"It's all right," Rebecca murmured to him when she hurried to his side. "We'll soon be home and you'll rest in your own lodge."

Tommy's large blue eyes examined her face. "He's worse, isn't he?"

Rebecca had to swallow the hard lump that formed in her throat. "I . . . can't tell in the dark. We'll have to wait." Wretchedly she turned her face away. "Yes, Tommy. Yes, he is. I'm afraid he's not going to make it."

Tears streamed down the white boy's face. "He has to, you hear? He *has to*!"

"Susssh, Tommy. Don't waken him, or get him upset. He has little enough strength as it is. Once we're in camp, we can get Tipsi some hot broth, fresh meat. Maybe the medicine man . . . can . . ."

"*I don't want him to die,*" Tommy sobbed in a ghastly voice. "He's my brother and I love him."

Rebecca halted the drag horse and hugged Tommy to her breast. "I know, Tommy, I know. We all love him. All we can do is our best—hope and trust that he'll come out of this."

"Don't you *see*?" Tommy protested. "We can't let him die like this."

"Be calm, my sweet one," Rebecca coaxed, caressing Tommy's hair. "The Sioux believe that thoughts can be transmitted. If you become convinced Tipsi will die, he'll react to it. Think strong thoughts and go back to sleep. I'll awaken you both when we reach the village."

Sadness blanketed the returning party as they entered the Red Top Lodge village. As news of the murder of White Buffalo Helps Him spread, women began to wail and the angry mutters of the warriors grew to a roar. Two Bulls called for an immediate council to open discussions on a new civil chief. Loudly mourning, the family of the slain leader protested the loss of Ptasan Okiye's body. How, they asked in confusion, could they prepare for a proper funeral and burial? Although grieving her father's death, Sweetgrass fainted away when she saw her son waxen and motionless on the travois. Tenderly, Tommy Archer lifted his friend and carried him into the lodge. The medicine man was summoned at once.

"C-can I stay with him?" Tommy asked timidly in Lakota. He displayed his right wrist and the thin right line of scab where it had been lightly cut. "He is my brother."

Sweetgrass had been revived by a whiff of juniper berry and looked hard at the white child before her. She saw not the light skin and near-white hair, but the hurt and worry in the big blue eyes and the true love of an Oglala that radiated from his pinched face. Burdened with all her sorrow, her heart went out to him.

"Yes, my second son. We will keep watch and pray with the *pezuta-wicaśa.*"

"Eh?" Tommy had heard the word for medicine man, as regards rituals and dance, but this new term evaded him.

"The healer, Tommy," Rebecca explained in English from over Tommy's shoulder. She went on in Lakota. "All of our hearts know sorrow, Sweeetgrass, for your father-in-law and your son. Tipsila . . . er, Capa acted bravely. He counted *coup* on the murderer. This one, Small Bear, counted *coup* also, and rescued your son when he fell to the gun-knife of the soldier."

The grieving mother's eyes lighted with this news. *"Hauhau!* You're brave and a warrior now. We must feast your heroic deed," she told Tommy.

"Not till Beaver's all well and can dance with me. *He's* the brave one. He nearly killed one of those who shot, aah . . ." In time Tommy remembered not to speak the name of the dead.

Watching the love that flowed from the distraught Oglala woman to Tommy Archer, Rebecca backed to the entrance of the lodge. "I'll go now."

Outside a different climate had come over the village. Shock, grief, and anger had hardened into icy determination. A shivery quiet spread outward from the center of the village to the furthest tipi. Near the council fire, Two Bulls sat astride his best war pony. He wore his war shirt and carried a long lance decorated with red feathers. *The red flag!* Rebecca thought with chilling precision. The call for total war.

"Onsimaya! Onsimaya, wakieunśa hiyupo, oglesaśa hiyupo, canumpahahśa hiyupo!" Face lined with the bitter grief of his father's death, he loudly issued his appeal. "I demand recognition," he repeated. "I demand recognition, come forward the deciders, come forward the red shirts, come forward the war pipe bearers!"

115

First to answer his call came the members of the Cante Tinza—Brave Heart—warrior society. Their leader took the red lance from Two Bulls and mounted his own war pony. Then he began to parade the war flag around the concentric rings of the village. Two large, deep-toned drums began to throb. Chanting, shouting for friends to join them, the Šayaota men fell in behind the Brave Hearts and started a shuffling dance as the procession serpentined through the dwellings. Two Bulls remained behind and signaled the elders and clan chiefs that the council would now begin.

From ahead came the pulse of the drums. Just like Injuns, Aaron Carter thought. When they weren't fightin' they were dancin' and stuffin' their guts. Well, they'd be eatin' lead before this night was over.

It had taken Ridgeway's hands all of the afternoon to chase half a dozen scrawny steers over into that big valley where the Oglala had their main camp. Carter and twenty of his "Range Detectives" had "tracked" the cattle here and now waited for full darkness before riding in to "arrest" the "rustlers." Exercising perhaps the poorest logic in a century, Carmoody had set the stage for this attack on the village for the very night that, unknown to him or his agents, the war drums throbbed and angry men gathered to paint their faces.

"There's an unusual large number of 'em down there," Brandy Parker suggested cautiously to his boss.

"All the more to shoot up," Aaron Carter replied lightly. "You aren't suggesting we can't handle a bunch of Injuns, are you?"

"Uh, no, Aaron. 'Course not. I just thought we might want to split up and hit 'em from two directions. Not take any chances on them gettin' behind us."

"Good idea." He turned to Colin Reese. "Col, take ten of the boys and ride around back o'the rim to the west side. Wait until ten minutes after full dark, then come stormin' down into the

116

village. We'll be doin' the same from here on the south. We'll pass through each other—an' be sure to tell the boys to be careful not to shoot any of our own—sweep the village and head out. By then, those cow-waddies will start off with the 'stolen' cattle an' drive 'em home."

"Just what does that accomplish?" a burly gunhawk named Miller asked doubtfully.

"Mr. Carmoody makes a full report to the Army about our findin' rustled cattle at the Oglala village. The soldier-boys will take it from there."

"And what do we get out of it?"

"A bonus if it works, Miller. An arrow up your ass if it doesn't."

It began as a low rumble that came from two directions. Rebecca Caldwell and several of the *akicita* heard it first. The camp police went out to investigate. They came back at a gallop moments later.

"*Wasicun!* They attack the camp!" came their shout of alarm.

Bemused, the braves exchanged eager smiles as they reached for their weapons. Many of them wondered how the white men had managed to deliver themselves at so opportune a time. Surely the Great Spirit had muddled their minds with a stirring stick. The moment of seeming slow-motion ended and the fighting men of the Šayaota scrambled to find advantageous positions to repel this attack.

Aaron Carter's men opened fire fifty yards from the first ring of lodges. Their slugs whacked noisily into the buffalo hide dwellings, harming little except the water-tight integrity of the tipis. Several paused to ignite torches. A mistake, since it made them excellent targets for the better marksmen among the Oglala.

Return fire came at once. A man with a flaming brand in his left hand cried out and flung the torch far from where he died.

117

Another kicked his mount to a gallop and rushed toward the camp. The mournful moan of fletchings cutting the air rose in front of him and he began to waver in the saddle.

Jerking erratically, his body held rigid against the pain, he cantered harmlessly into the village, six arrows decorating his chest and abdomen. His eyes quickly glazed and he toppled from his mount when young White Willow struck him with her root gouging stick. She jumped back in time to avoid the rush of another yelling white man.

Before Brandy Parker could blast White Willow into oblivion, he came into the sight picture of Rebecca Caldwell's Winchester. Her finger tightened on the trigger and a .44-40 slug slammed into the side of Parker's head. Another round drove him from atop his horse and under hoof, to be pulped into unrecognizable gore. In his last dying instant, he realized how valid his complaint had been.

Shouts and gunshots came from every direction. Here and there, warriors pulled their enemies down from their horses, to smash at them with stone clubs. Imperceptibly at first, the fighting dwindled. The sound of hoofs pounding away in the distance indicated that some of the attackers had escaped. Near the central fire ring, four white men, their ammunition exhausted, were held at bay by a ring of hard-faced warriors.

"Don't kill them," Rebecca called in Lakota. "We can get answers from them."

"Who's she?" Theron Miller asked Aaron Carter.

"Don't know. We got enough problems as it is."

"We ain't gonna fight our way outta this," Colin Reese observed nervously.

"For certain sure," Carter agreed. "So we die tryin'. It's that or be tortured by the Sioux."

Rebecca Caldwell stalked forward, her rifle slantwise across her body, each step radiating power and authority. "You men. Surrender and you won't be harmed. We want to know who sent you. Why did you attack the village?"

"You can go to hell, you half-breed bitch!" Colin Reese snarled.

"That's not nice," Rebecca returned calmly. "Do you really want me to let these warriors have some sport with you? They won't kill you right away, of course, but you'll wish they had."

"Just like a damned half-breed. Crazy as a loon," Reese snarled.

Methodically, Rebecca brought up her Winchester and shot Theron Miller through the calf. He howled with pain and fell to the ground.

"What did you do that for, you crazy bitch?" Reese screamed.

"I didn't want anyone to think I'd shot you because you made me mad," she answered matter-of-factly. "You see my point, though? You don't have to be killed to be taken captive. The condition you are in is up to you."

Aaron Carter shrugged in resignation. "What is it you want to know, lady?"

"Who set this up?"

"Alystaire Carmoody," Carter answered.

"Why?"

"It's a good thing you're boss, Carter," Reese snarled. "Mr. Carmoody can't have our hides for *you* rattin' out like this."

Rebecca coolly shot off the toe of Reese's right boot. "Just like mules," she stated flatly. "Some you can teach with kindness. Others take force. Why did this Alystaire Carmoody send you here?"

In clear, terse words, Carter described the phony rustling scheme and the involvement of Grover Ridgeway's ranch hands. He concluded by explaining how their attack was supposed to be an attempt to arrest the rustlers.

"What did Carmoody expect to gain from that?"

"To stir up trouble, so the Army would drive the Sioux out," came Carter's sullen reply.

"What business is that of Carmoody's?"

"The land. He's president of the Dakota Cattlemen's Association. They want to carve up the territory between the big shots. We all got a little stake in it."

"What about the governor?"

"Hell, when they take over, they'll replace that fat fool with one of their own," Carter responded confidently.

Rebecca paused a moment, considering. "What if I were to get you out of here with your hair still in place? Would you be willing to repeat all of this to the governor?"

"You bet I would," Carter agreed, seeing life where a moment before there had been certain death.

"You rotten turncoat, you'll not live to enjoy it," Reese hissed.

"If you force me to fire another shot, mister, I'll use it to blow off your balls," Rebecca declared in a tone of sweet reason. To Carter she offered, "There's a man here who can take you to Pierre. You'll be in custody, of course. It's Philo Bates, the U.S. marshal. Do you agree to go along with him and to tell everything to the governor?"

Aaron Carter looked around at the menacing ring of Oglala warriors. He licked dry lips and nodded solemnly. "You bet I will. I ain't ready to die slow over a Sioux fire for the likes of Alystaire Carmoody."

Philo Bates pushed forward out of the crowd that had gathered. "I'll be ready to leave at first light. It'll take a couple of days to get to Pierre. I only got two sets of cuffs and leg irons along, so I'll take your parole now if you'll give it, sincerely-like," he told Aaron Carter.

"You might as well," Rebecca said. "Because there'll be an escort of Cante Tinzas along."

"Can-te—whats?"

"Strong Hearts," Rebecca clarified. "The warrior society. One little slip and ziiiiit! You'll be able to swallow your coffee six inches lower than usual."

"Awh, they won't be any trouble, Miss Rebecca," Bates told her. He took time to expel a long stream of tobacco juice. "I ain't never lost a prisoner yet. I brought some of 'em in alive, but I brüng 'em all in just the same. I'll see they tell their story to a territorial judge and to the governor."

"I'll count on that, Philo. That might be the break we need."

"Not when Mr. Carmoody finds out," Colin Reese growled ominously.

Chapter 13

A sibilant rustle came from the tortoiseshell rattle, and vapors from a smoldering bunch of fresh herbs wafted across the still face of the child, propelled by an eagle wing fan. Crouched low, the healer of the Red Top Lodge people chanted in a low voice while he studied the waxen pallor of Tipsila Ce's skin.

The bluish, puckered lips of the wound had an angry red circle around each puncture. The soldier's gun-knife had pierced through skin and baby-fat on the boy's side. Had it pierced the abdomen as well? This Heron Leg knew no more surely than Rebecca Caldwell had on the trail. From among his paraphernalia, Heron Leg selected a long, thin bone pipe. One end had been cut diagonally and sharpened to a point, though its inside diameter remained the same as the opposite tip. Heron Leg felt the heat of corruption when he laid his fingers alongside the entry point. Now was the time.

He put the blunt end of the pipe in his mouth and with his free hand wiped away the crust of scab. Sticky yellow fluid seeped out, a faint odor of putrification accompanying it. Its scent brought a frown to the healing medicine man's forehead. Now he removed the bone pipe from his mouth and pressed it gently into the wound.

Although comatose, Tipsila Ce winced away from the pain

and whimpered softly. His breathing rate faltered, ceased, then resumed, lighter and faster. Of course he felt it, poor little fellow, Heron Leg thought. He daren't apply a draught for pain relief, not with the boy unconscious. Gritting his teeth against the pain he willingly took unto himself, Heron Leg pushed the pipe further into the opening. Fully half its length slid into Tipsila Ce's body before he ceased. He gave it a slow turn of one hundred eighty degrees.

Bending low, Heron Leg applied his lips to the blunt end and began to suck. He nearly gagged as his mouth filled with pus. When he'd drawn a satisfactory amount, he ceased and carefully spat the result into the palm of one hand. This he thoroughly examined before rinsing his mouth. His stomach heaved and hot bile rose in his throat. Despite the unpleasant sensations, he felt encouragement. Once more he closed his lips over the pipe.

Another stream of viscous putrescence squirted into his mouth. But, he noted exultantly when he examined it, not a bit of the greenish amber fluid of the abdominal cavity. The wound, though rotting like too-old meat, had not entered a vital portion of the boy's body. If he had some means of stopping the increase of infection, he could save the child's life.

Outside, he maintained his somber expression, in keeping with the news he had to impart to the anxious mother and those keeping vigil with her. "It's a close thing. There is not a hole to his center. That means he can live. There is much fire and stinking ooze. That means he might die. Bring me red willow bark, sage, and the white man's make-clean grease."

Several of the curious hurried to obey him. Others remained to gossip of the attack. Heron Leg had heard the shooting and cries of alarm. Intent on his task as healer, he had ignored them to continue his work. Antelope Runner, still bloodstained from battle, came to inquire of his son.

"It's no different than before," Rebecca regretfully told him. "Except that we know he wasn't stabbed far enough

124

toward his middle to go into the belly."

"I'm relieved. Will he live?"

"No one knows."

"There are wounded to care for," Antelope Runner told Heron Leg.

"Others can do that. I stay with your son."

"I am grateful, Healer. Do your best."

"I am, my friend, I am."

Rebecca walked away with Antelope Runner. Everywhere they heard angry mutters against the whites. Little damage had been done. Two Bulls stood outside the council lodge. His face wore a grim mask.

"The white men have given us our answer," he said in a flat tone. "There's little left to decide."

"It will be war?" Rebecca asked, not doubting the outcome.

"It's for the council to decide."

"I want to try something to prevent needless bloodshed," Rebecca offered.

"You can do nothing."

"Two Bulls . . . never mind. Have you seen Lone Wolf?"

"He's over there."

Rebecca found her longtime companion between two tipis, looking both amused and concerned. With him was Tommy Archer, quite pale and shaken, a greenish tinge around his lips. When Rebecca put a hand on his bare shoulder, the boy shivered violently.

"What's the matter, Tommy?"

"I—I, uh, k-k-killed a man," he stammered. "H-h-he was tryin' to stick a knife in a little girl. I shot him-m-m-m in the face. It blew off the b-back of his head." Tommy whirled away to bend over and heave up on a dry stomach.

"Oh, you poor thing," Rebecca consoled, sensitive to the child's anguish.

Two Bulls had walked up during Tommy's explantion. His eyes glowed with pride. "My son is very brave," he declared in a rumble, aware of the cause of this little scene. "First he counts *coup* on a soldier inside their war camp, next he saves the life of his friend, then he kills his first man. Not twelve summers and he's already a warrior."

Bent over, still holding his sore belly, Tommy spoke in a weak voice. "Bein' a warrior ain't all that neat."

Now Rebecca understood the humor that Lone Wolf saw in the situation. She, too, produced a smile and ruffled Tommy's hair. "You're Mahtociqala, Small Bear, not some sissy white boy. Your new father's proud of you; we are, too."

"I never knew there was s-so much *blood* inside a person," Tommy cried in misery. "Or so many brains. Ugh!"

"You saved a child's life. Twice now."

In a flash, Tommy's expression changed. "Beaver? How is he?"

"No different. At least he hasn't gotten worse," Rebecca hurried to assure him. "Now, go get something to eat, then get some sleep."

Tommy's stricken expression brought another smile to Rebecca's lips. "*Eat!* How could anyone eat after that?"

"You'd better, or you'll have a stomach ache all night," the white squaw advised.

"Uh . . . I do feel sorta empty."

"Go on, then. Now, Lone Wolf, I have an idea," Rebecca began as Tommy trotted off.

"What about?"

"There's little chance of preventing a general uprising now that those idiots attacked this village. It's not just the hotheads calling for war with all whites. What we need is more leverage to force some action against this Cattlemen's Association and compel the Army to change its policy. According to what Aaron Carter said, this Grover Ridgeway sounds like a weak link. I want to know more about him, what he really feels. The best place to do that is at his ranch. If I can arrange to meet Ridgeway and then fix it to get access to his records, we might find us someone willing to cooperate."

"That's ridiculous," Lone Wolf exploded. "What chance

126

would you have? And how much time would all this take?"

"Not long, I imagine. It's a safe enough plan. Besides, what other choice do we have?"

"I don't like it," Lone Wolf returned stubbornly.

"I don't either. So tell me another way?"

"You're here earlier than I expected, Alystaire," Col. Bryce Peyton greeted him as his friend entered the office at Camp Cullen.

"Well, I got paid sooner than expected for those, ah, extra cattle. Thought you'd appreciate having your share early on."

"I do, and that's a fact. Brandy?"

"Before Retreat formation?" Carmoody asked in feigned surprise.

"Why the hell not? Grant took a snort with his breakfast coffee. He got to be president. Say when. . . ."

Peyton poured from a cut-glass decanter he had taken from a closed cupboard built into one wall. While he did so, Carmoody produced an envelope, thickly padded with U.S. banknotes. This he dropped on the colonel's desk.

"There's a little bonus in there, too. We managed to unload some of that alkali ground out in the Bad Lands on some eastern dudes."

"Hummm. A nice little nest egg, Alystaire. It will surely help my retirement. But I'm afraid the Army's no longer going to be able to help you seize land from the Indians for our mutual profit."

Carmoody frowned. "Why's that?"

"We're coming under considerable scrutiny from headquarters. There was a, ah, shooting here the other day. . . ."

"I heard about that," Carmoody responded dryly. "No loss gettin' rid of that stubborn old fart, White Buffalo."

"It is when someone manages to report that he was unarmed when killed," Peyton snapped back.

"Who'd be fool enough to do that?"

127

"A young officer named Larsen. Seems he's got religion lately when it comes to Indians. Has a lot of friends on this post, I gather. Enough so's one or more of them got word to department headquarters about what went on here. Now I'm at a considerable disadvantage. There'll be an inspector general team down here within a week."

"What about this Larsen?"

"Quite a pity, really. He, ah, hanged himself in his cell last night."

Carmoody smacked his lips and slapped one ham hand on his fat thigh. "In for a penny, in for a pound, I say. But won't that, ah, alleviate your situation somewhat?"

"These accommodations are distasteful, to say the least. One never wishes to become beholden to, ah, others. Such arrangements frequently become expensive."

"All the more reason why you should make use of your position to acquire more funds. We've got the Sioux stirred up nicely for you. It won't take much more to give you free rein to exterminate them. After that, we cut this territory up to suit ourselves."

"Not with an inspector general looking over my shoulder. No, Alystaire, I'm afraid my involvement in this is definitely at an end."

"It had better not be," Carmoody snapped, face hard, small pig eyes glittering. "There's that little matter of three unaccounted-for killings a couple of years ago. And all the land deals so far."

Peyton's eyes dulled and his chest sank in resignation. "And here I was worried about my assistants of the past night. It's always your closest friends who can do you the greatest harm, I suppose."

Carmoody's porcine features rearranged themselves into false good will. "Come now, Bryce. I don't wish to cause you any discomfort or embarrassment. Hardly would I want to see you standing in the dock, accused of heinous crimes. It's for your own good, as well as mine and that of the Association.

Without your frequent and wholehearted assistance we could never pull this off. You will reconsider, won't you?"

"I, uh, seem to have no choice."

"Of course, you do. They say Leavenworth has a remarkable climate. Now, shall we have some more of that brandy and toast our continued good fortune?"

Despite everyone's advice to the contrary, Rebecca made ready for a journey to Murdo, the small town nearest to Grover Ridgeway's ranch. The council still met, debated, expostulated, yet had not come to a firm decision. Rebecca inclined toward believing the result was preordained. In light of this, she felt it necessary to undertake the dangerous, and probably unproductive, journey to try to compromise Grover Ridgeway's secrets.

"You'll be careful?" Lone Wolf urged.

"Don't be a mother hen. I can take care of myself. I will also contact a doctor and ask about the type of wound Tipsi has."

"That's my good gal," Lone Wolf offered in conciliation.

"There's something in writing somewhere," Rebecca returned to the main topic in an attempt to convince herself every bit as much as the doubters. "Something that will compel the territorial government to act. And since there is, *has* to be, I'll find it."

Chapter 14

From inside the town, Murdo, Dakota Territory appears to have been built on a hillside. The illusion is successfully deceptive. Actually, Murdo was constructed on the slope of a gigantic gully. The high, flat terrain surrounding the hamlet, better than two thousand feet in altitude, had been gashed open here and there by a whim of nature. Over the eons, water courses had formed and enlarged on the openings. Ultimately, men had come seeking gold and stayed to make their homes. Rebecca Caldwell's arrival in the community created little stir. At least, until after she had registered at the small hotel and prepared herself for the role she would play.

Dressed in a tiered silk dress picked out with bits of lace and voile, her raven locks done in an upsweep that left three short sausage curls dangling at the back, at once severe and provocative, she made her "entrance" into Murdo society. In the lobby bar, she struck up a conversation with a well-dressed man of middle years, while the desk clerk gawked at the transition effected in one short hour.

"I'm simply *dyin'* to meet him, you see," Rebecca effused in a carefully maintained southern accent. "My daddy, P.G. Waterhouse, of the Savannah Waterhouses, told me that since I insisted on visiting Cousin Arnell in Dakota Territory, I absolutely *must* come to Murdo and talk to Grover Ridgeway."

Rebecca had done some quick research before departing Pierre for Murdo. Grover Ridgeway was considered, according to *Country Gentleman* magazine, the formost experimental breeder of shorthorn cattle west of the Mississippi. The name Percival Waterhouse, and that of his daughter, Samantha, had been plucked from the same source. A little additional reading had provided her a wide, if shallow, knowledge of the new rage in animal husbandry, shorthorn cattle.

Imported from England, the Aberdeen and Herfordshire strains had become popular in the eastern and southern states. Several bold cattlemen on the plains, premier among them Grover Ridgeway, had undertaken to introduce them where previously only the buffalo and wild Texas longhorn had held sway. Lacking any better means of making Ridgeway's acquaintance, Rebecca had assumed the persona of Samantha Waterhouse. Now she waited anxiously for the hoped-for introduction.

"You've come to the right person," Miles Pendleton responded. "I count myself as one of Grover's closer friends. Of course, while you were in Pierre, you should have looked up Alystaire Carmoody. He an' Grover are like that." Pendleton illustrated his point with thumb and index finger pressed tightly together. "The Slash-R-Bar is just ten miles south of here on the Little White River. Grover's due in town today or tomorrow. We have some business over at the bank. I'm sure he'd offer you the hospitality of his spread."

"Ooh, I just knew you were the right man to help a lady in distress. Will Mr. Ridgeway be staying at the hotel, too?"

"No. He has a small town house he maintains for such visits. Rest assured, Miss Samantha, when he arrives, I'll make it a point to introduce you."

"Thank you so much, Mr. Pendleton. I simply don't know how to express my gratitude."

A twinkle in his far-seeing gray eyes under bushy white brows, Pendleton took her small, graceful hand in both of his. "You could consent to grace my table tonight at dinner," he suggested.

"Why, I declare, I'd be delighted, Mr. Pendleton. But . . ." she pouted prettily, "you simply must promise to visit us at Balmoral down in Geo'gia. How else can I repay the obligations I'm accumulating through your kindness?"

"Think nothing of it, my dear. It would be my pleasure. Perhaps your father would enjoy riding to the hounds?"

Rebecca could not resist at least one little tweak to cap her performance and hopefully add credibility to it. Accordingly, she produced a small moue of displeasure and wrinkled her brow.

"Daddy's never held much stock in the hunt. 'Why should two dozen grown men, on big, strong horses chase that poor little red critter until his tongue's hanging out and his tail's draggin',' he always says."

Eager to be ingratiating, Miles Pendleton arranged his mood accordingly. "Capital, I say. Of course, we New Englanders never did see the reason behind that particular sport. It would pleasure me just to see his remarkable livestock. Well then, until this evening?"

"This evening, Mr. Pendleton. A late supper?"

"Exactly. Say . . . nine o'clock?"

"I'll be waiting."

Bryce Peyton sat in his darkening office, his long, spatulate fingers laced over his slight paunch. His mustache ends drooped as dramatically as his spirits. As he had done each day since Alystaire Carmoody's visit, he reviewed in his mind every nuance of their conversation. True to Carmoody's prediction, the murder of Arnulf Larsen had come back to haunt him. He could no longer deny that. Loyalty alone had not purchased silence. He had been shattered to learn that only the previous day.

That was when he had discovered the crudely lettered note in the upper drawer of his desk.

LEVE $1,000 IN BANKNOTES IN THIS DRAR ON
WENSDAY. DO IT OR THEYEL NO ABOUT HOW
LARSEN DIED.

Only, who was the extortionist? Was it fat Sergeant
Dumont, the provost sergeant? Or Corporal Banner, who had
used his brawny strength to haul the knotted blanket over the
barred door frame and tie it off, while Larsen struggled. It had
to be one of them; only they knew. Either way, he'd find out
before long. He had made a show of retiring to his quarters
early. Then he had slipped back here while the men ate their
evening meal. He didn't expect a visit until well after Taps. His
suspects' duties with the guard mount would allow them to
move about then without drawing undue attention. Then greed
would get its just reward.

Greed, Peyton thought giddily, unaware that his mind
hovered on the edge of hysteria. Simple greed would be the
death of someone tonight. He didn't really care which one it
turned out to be. He would have to arrange some sort of
"desertion," of course. Only this time he would work alone.
Nervously he fingered the keen edge of the big Sheffield Bowie.

It had been a long time since he had killed with cold steel.
For a frightened moment, Bryce Peyton wondered if he could
do so again. His career, his reputation, his very life all pivoted
on this one night and the bloody deed he contemplated. But,
could he do it?

A creaky board, outside in the sergeant major's office, gave
him his answer. Fired with new resolve, Bryce Peyton shrank
back into the dark shadows beside the regimental colors. He
held the knife low and ready. He'd soon know the identity of
his blackmailer and seal his lips forever. The door opened a
crack. Peyton had tensed to the point of trembling. The thin
portal swung wider.

With a furtive rush, a vaguely familiar figure entered the
room. Without hesitation, the darker mass moved to the desk,
slid open the top drawer. Bryce Peyton took his first step

forward, the knife poised to strike. The intruder stiffened for an instant, then whirled around.

"Hello, Colonel," Captain Stanley the provost marshal, said in his burry, adenoidal voice.

"Duncan Stanley!" Peyton exploded, barely above a whisper. "How? Why—you?"

"Put down the knife, Colonel. It would hardly do for you to dispose of one of your officers. And in such a messy manner, at that. As to the how and why, it's simple. Uh, d'you mind if I sit down?"

His body still charged with adrenalin, his purpose thwarted, Bryce Peyton had reached a state of befuddlement. He waved vaguely at a chair. Captain Stanley seated himself primly, properly erect, hands on the creases of his trousers where they bisected his thighs.

"Of late I've found myself unable to sleep well at night. I get up and roam. As provost marshal there's never a report on the watch sheet. I happened to be outside the cell block when our Lieutenant Larsen met his demise. That's how. Even you should know the why. Army pay is hardly sufficient to live on. I detest poverty and the prospect of a future that offers little else. I've been aware for some time that you have been receiving a, uh, stipend for certain advantageous services rendered to your friend Alystaire Carmoody. Why not, I asked myself, arrange to receive a share in this largess?"

Still unable to fathom this unexpected turn, Peyton muttered, "But the note . . ."

"Ah, the note. Obviously done by a barely literate person. I thought that a clever touch. Though now it appears that I took you too much for granted. Your thought process must have run something like this: 'Anyone that illiterate must be stupid enough to fall into a clever trap, provided it's baited properly.' Eh? Isn't that it, Colonel?"

Duncan Stanley's bantering mood drove a goad into him. Bryce Peyton's face flushed with hot crimson and he remembered the knife in his hand. "Don't patronize me. I still

135

have your life in my hands."

"Oooh," Stanley replied lazily. "I thought we'd dispensed with that long ago. Now, let's get down to terms. I won't be greedy, uh—at least, not too greedy. The demand for a thousand was to flush you out, confirm our bargaining ground, so to speak. What I want is five hundred now. Then, as the need arises, you'll be called upon for additional contributions. Call it your participation in my retirement fund, if you will."

"This is outrageous!" Peyton expostulated in a harsh whisper.

"Murdering poor Lieutenant Larsen was outrageous, I would say."

"You bastard."

"Call me what you will, just so long as the donations are made promptly. Oh, ah, and by the way, Colonel. I have taken the precaution of writing everything down, as an eye-witness to your, er, indiscretion. All properly attested to. In the event of my sudden death or disappearance, it will be delivered into the hands of the proper authorities. Now then, when will you have the five hundred dollars ready for me?"

Crushed by the terrible reality of his undeniable guilt and its exposure, Bryce Peyton surrendered without condition. His words came out in a strangled rasp. "Tomorrow morning, after officers' call."

Two days passed in relative boredom for Rebecca Caldwell before Grover Ridgeway arrived in Murdo. During that time she had become accustomed to the idea that the rancher's headquarters lay not more than twenty miles from the Sayaota village. She eagerly dressed and assumed her impersonation of Samantha Waterhouse when Miles Pendleton called at her room to inform her that Ridgeway had invited them both to join him for a later supper at his town house.

Surprise turned to keen interest for Rebecca when she discovered Grover Ridgeway to be much younger than she had envisioned. At thirty-two he retained his hard, slender figure, his shoulders broad and square, eyes bright with the glow of his special vision. He engulfed her slim hand in both his huge ones when they were introduced, grinning in that way of a man who truly appreciates quality, in livestock or in people. His six-foot height carried his weight well, almost to the point of making him appear thin. His rich voice sent shivers along Rebecca's spine.

"You are most welcome, Miss Waterhouse. We Westerners rarely stand on such formality, you'll soon learn. If you'll promise to call me Grover, I'll take the liberty of addressing you by your Christian name."

"Sam," Rebecca replied. "I prefer Sam. That's what my dear ol' daddy calls me. Sort of makes up for not havin' a son, don't you see?" She dimpled and dipped her head demurely.

"But I understood that Percival Waterhouse had two sons," Ridgeway returned, surprised.

Caught out, Rebecca thought in a moment of panic. Then she regained her composure. "That's quite right. Though it pains us to think of it lately. The War, you know. One of my brothers fought for the No'th. The other for the Cause. Hiram is still alive, though Daddy's disowned him for turning his coat. David died fighting for southern freedom."

"I, er, see. Enough of this unpleasant topic. Come into the parlor. Would you take sherry, Sam?"

"Why, thank you, Grover, I would."

"Miles, bourbon and branch for you?"

"Like usual, Grover. I ain't changed since I could lift the glass."

Dinner turned out to be excellent. From soup to after-dinner drinks, Rebecca's tasting strongly of coffee, each dish had been planned to complement those that went before and came after. Rebecca ascribed it all to Grover Ridgeway's being a man of culture. His refinement and taste showed in the decor of his part-time home, his selection of food and drink, and the smooth quality of his conversation.

"Do you like it?" Ridgeway impinged on her contemplation.

"Oh, yes. Quite . . . different."

"It's from Mexico. Made from fermented and distilled coffee beans and brandy. I hope that it, and the meal, have your stamp of approval, Sam."

Rebecca gave him her most intimate of smiles. "Oh, they both do, Grover. Your appointments here show such attention to detail, I wonder what your ranch is like?"

"You'll soon find out, provided you accept my invitation. Oh, not for a mere visit. Miles has already offered to escort you to the Slash-R-Bar. I mean to have you come for a prolonged stay, to get to know the ranch and me a lot better."

"Why, goodness me, I'd be delighted. Daddy did so want to learn of your success with shorthorns."

"Then it's settled?"

This decision had come upon her far sooner than Rebecca had prepared for. She batted her eyes, relying on the southern belle personality to carry her while she organized her thoughts. It would be immensely useful to her plans. There appeared little risk. No one of Grover Ridgeway's obvious stature could think of a woman as an agent seeking incriminating evidence. She lowered her chin slightly and allowed the sausage curls to bob in a demure fashion.

"When would we be departing?"

"Our affairs should be settled up some time tomorrow, right Miles? In which case, we could leave for the ranch the next morning."

"You western men are so bold, so, ah, decisive. I can't for the life of me find any objection. I'll be ready when you wish to go."

Chapter 15

With a final flurry of three muted beats, the drums went silent. Throughout the Red Top Lodge encampment, people waited anxiously to hear the announcement that would come from the council tipi. For a long while they remained in suspense. A ripple of conversation radiated outward when the door flap swung away and Two Bulls came out, to stand at one side. Hump, a man of fifty summers, appeared next and took a place on the opposite side. A mutter of consternation came from the onlookers.

"The council remains of two minds," Standing Elk declared when he exited and stood between the two men. "Half of the deciders are behind Two Bulls for chief." A ragged cheer went up, and Small Bear was first to run to take a place beside his adopted father.

"Half speak for Hump to be chief." Another expression of approval filled the air, while supporters jostled to find a place on that side of the lodge.

"Hump speaks for peace," Standing Elk went on. "Two Bulls for war."

Loud whoops came from the younger warriors, who hurried to place themselves in Two Bulls's ranks. The old people, the wives and mothers, and many children streamed the other way. When the milling subsided, equal numbers of warriors—who, after all, were the only ones who counted—represented the diverging opinions. Another stalemate.

"Will one man speak for peace? Will one for war?" Standing Elk seemed unduly perplexed, though many knew the reason for his concern.

No one moved. "There can't be two chiefs within our band," Standing Elk pleaded.

Mothers in the peace faction pleaded with their sons. Sons urged their fathers to come across. Scornfully aloof at first, some of the young braves began to call to wives and children. Slowly a shifting began. Total numbers changed, but the count of warriors on each side remained the same. The realization of what this impasse meant dawned on some of those with older memories. Gray-headed women began to wail.

"*Tikahpa!*" Two Bulls called out in a commanding bass. "*Tikahpa!*"

Tipi down, strike camp! The dread order had been given.

Two Bulls's followers hurried about to follow the directive. A bee swarm hum filled the air with the sound of mourning. The band had been divided. Members of the same family would become as strangers. They would live apart. Ancient legend dictated that surely a great disaster would follow.

Only, for whom?

"Why, I declare that's the most beautiful house I've ever seen," Rebecca Caldwell announced when she first saw Grover Ridgeway's home.

"Grover's quite proud of it," Miles Pendleton replied from beside her on the buggy seat.

Ridgeway had expended every effort in the construction of the stone mansion. His dedication had made the southern-plantation-style edifice look entirely at home on the harsh prairie. Tall porticoes, supported by white columns, a wide veranda, Federal period capitals over the tall, narrow, lead-glassed windows, and a domed cupola with a weather vane, markedly Jeffersonian in design and surmounting all, blended together harmoniously. The Slash-R-Bar headquarters turned out to be a showplace. Everywhere, Rebecca saw the ranch brand, /R—, wrought in iron or burned into wood. Lines of young cottonwoods separated the manse from the outbuildings.

Among those, Rebecca noted a stable, two white-painted barns, equipment sheds, a granary, a blacksmith shop, and a bunkhouse. Smoke rose from the chimney of a separate building that served as cookhouse for the ranch hands. Chickens fluttered in the yard, and from a small pond, aggressive geese came honking and hissing to give the alarm at their approach.

"They're better than dogs for Indians," Pendleton laughingly told her. "All that hissing and weaving around scares them outta their, ah, moccasins. It gives good warning, too."

"If you don't get used to it," Rebecca responded. "Daddy had to dispose of all our geese. They made no distinction between our nigrahs and some prowler. Fortunately, they're good eating."

Pendleton laughed heartily. "Mrs. Stout is going to love you," he managed at last. "She sees the goose population around here in the same light. 'Ought to have one every Christmas', is the way she puts it. 'And any other time the notion strikes.' She's a caution. I always feel good visiting here."

"It's such a lovely place to come to," Rebecca replied sincerely.

At a distance the ranch house had looked splendid, up close it was magnificent. Rebecca felt completely overawed.

Uniformed servants awaited them and they bowed obsequiously when Miles Pendleton halted the buggy under the vaulted portico. Grover Ridgeway, who had come ahead of them, appeared in the tall doorway, dressed in casual, yet costly, clothing. Beside him a short, stout, big-bosomed woman with a full head of gray-streaked black hair beamed her welcome in a wide, generous smile. Pendleton dismounted and handed Rebecca down, then a lad of fourteen or so led the team away.

"Welcome to my modest home," Grover Ridgeway boomed as he started down the steps.

"Law, but I'm overwhelmed," Rebecca Caldwell replied in her guise of Samantha Waterhouse. "It's all . . . simply gorgeous."

"Thank you. That's the most sincere compliment I've recieved. Sam, I want you to meed Mrs. Stout. Agatha, this is Samantha Waterhouse. She'll be our guest for as long as she wishes."

Agatha Stout patted at the large, tight bun in which she habitually wore her hair and came forward. "How do you do, Miss Samantha? I've had a nice room prepared for you." Her open, candid blue eyes twinkled with merriment. "Now, if you're like Mr. Grover's other visitors, you'll be wanting to remove a bit of dust and have a light snack. It will be ready for you on the south veranda in twenty minutes. Charles!" she snapped at a young man in a house boy's livery. "Take Miss Samantha's luggage and show her to her quarters."

"Yes, ma'am." There was no question that Agatha Stout ran this house.

Ridgeway patted Rebecca's hand and nodded to Pendleton. "We'll join you for tea, Sam," he stated, being, like the others, under Agatha Stout's command.

Rebecca found her room to be bright and airy. Paper, with a pattern of flocked bluebells, covered the walls above a low wainscoting of some light, fine-grained wood. Pink rosebuds decorated the pitcher and the rim of the washbasin, and a huge bloom filled the bottom of the latter. They sat on top of a cabinet that sported twin towel racks and contained a chamber pot with the same floral pattern. A canopied bed had been turned down invitingly. She longed for a luxurious stretch and a short nap. No time, though. Mrs. Stout awaited her.

She removed her dusty outer garments and washed her

hands and face, then opened a portmanteau and took out a fresh dress. For a moment, as she slid it on, Rebecca felt the mild discomfort she experienced whenever she had to wear white women's clothing. It passed as she fastened the last button and stepped to the hall door.

"You look lovely," Grover Ridgeway declared as both gentlemen stood to acknowledge her arrival.

"Thank you, Grover. It's just a little something I have for informal wear."

"Out here," Ridgeway confided, "informal wear is generally a flannel shirt, whipcord trousers and boots. Ah! Here comes Charles with what I'm sure will be a mountain of Agatha's delicacies."

Charles pushed a heavy-laden cart, which contained a wooden bucket of cold well water, in which reposed bottles of beer, with glasses and decanters of sherry, bourbon, and brandy, three large, dome-covered trays, and a formal tea service. When he removed the first cover, the savory aroma of roast beef rose from diamond-cut sandwiches. In the center was a molded mound of homemade cottage cheese, bordered by glistening peach halves. The second lid revealed an assortment of cheeses and crackers. The third platter carried a wide variety of tiny pastries, sweets, and trifles.

"No one, not even your Mrs. Stout, could have whipped this up in twenty minutes," Rebecca observed, impressed by the care and quality of their afternoon repast.

"Truth to tell," Ridgeway admitted as he helped himself to a plate full of the remarkable array, "she's been at it since yesterday. But mind you, she'll not let anyone else touch her creations except to stir the pot or remove something from the oven."

"She is, ah, a bit formidable," Rebecca replied.

"She's a gem. Now, help yourself. What would you like to drink? Tea?"

"A beer, I think. Then tea with my pastry."

"There's no surer sign of good health, and good sense, than a hearty appetite," Miles Pendleton said through a chuckle.

"Miles is an advocate of food as a means to long life. Also, he's fortifying himself for the ride back to town."

Rebecca made a face. "You're leaving so soon?"

"I have to. But I'll be back for the party this weekend."

"Ah, pardon me, which party?"

"It was to be a surprise, but big-mouth here let it slip," Ridgeway injected. "I'm having a party to welcome you to the Slash-R-Bar."

"Why, that's so kind. It's as though I've come to stay."

"You can. As I told Agatha, you're our guest for as long as you wish."

Rebecca read the deeper meaning in the tone of Grover's voice. His intense gaze and charged aura conveyed an interest in her beyond courtesy to the daughter of a fellow cattle breeder. Despite herself, she recognized the heightening of her own emotions. Young and handsome. Both words quite comfortably fit Grover Ridgeway. For a moment she found it hard to believe he was supposed to be mixed up in something shady, if not totally illegal.

"Well then," and she found it hard to speak, "I suppose I can rearrange my schedule to include more time at this wonderful planta . . . er, ranch of yours, Grover."

Pleasure bloomed on Ridgeway's face and he seemed . . . relieved? "Good. We'll count on that. I'm sorry you have to eat and run, Miles. Agatha has laid on a truly extraordinary dinner for tonight."

Pendleton rubbed his burgeoning paunch. "*I'd* love it, but my waistline would suffer. All the same, I'll see you two on Saturday."

"Thank you so much for all you've done for me, Mr. Pendleton," Rebecca said sincerely, rising to wish him farewell.

"Until Saturday, Miss Samantha."

*   *   *

Dinner lived up to Grover Ridgeway's advance praise. With Miles Pendleton gone, it became a small, intimate late supper. It featured warm slices of wild duck breast in a sharp sauce and a number of side dishes. Conversation with Grover kept Rebecca from recalling exactly what their fare had consisted of. Ridgeway spoke of his cattle and the success he had enjoyed in developing a hardy strain of shorthorn that thrived on prairie grass, with only a minimum of time graining them before shipping to market. Then their talk turned personal.

Rebecca discovered that Ridgeway was a widower, with sons of twelve and fourteen. Both boys rode with the ranch hands, now off in the northern pastures, rounding up cattle for the winter range close to headquarters. He seemed so young to be a father of two and a widower. It made him a bit more vulnerable. Before they parted for the evening, Rebecca agreed to go riding the next day, to see part of the ranch. It had been a most pleasant encounter, and her only gloomy thought centered on the likelihood of having to endure a sidesaddle in order to maintain her impersonation.

At nine the next morning, Ridgeway surprised and pleased her by bringing around a shiny dark Arabian with a stockman's saddle. "We haven't had a sidesaddle around the place since Cynthia died," he explained apologetically. "I hope you won't mind."

"Oh, not at all. Often when Daddy's not at home I ride English saddle. To be frank, and I hope not too risqué, sidesaddles tend to chafe in the most uncomfortable places."

Laughing, they mounted up and cantered away from the stable. They headed northward, along the angling bank of the Little White River. The pace was such that it permitted them to converse easily.

"The hands will be back by Friday. You'll meet my boys."

"They're a little young to be working cowboys, aren't they?"

"True, but I've so few hands on this time of year. Don't worry about them, about getting along. I'm sure they'll be every bit as enchanted as I am."

He'd said it gently and with a ring of sincerity that Rebecca could not deny. A fleeting, shy smile accompanied the declaration. Stifling her feminine reactions, she decided to probe a bit.

"You have such a large bunkhouse, I naturally assumed you employed a great number."

"Oh, I do. In the spring for round-up and branding, and the drive to market. Right now I'm doubly short-handed. Some of my men are working with the Association Range Detectives."

"Trouble with cattle thieves?"

"Rustling is not uncommon around here."

"What about Indians? I heard in Pierre that the Association, ah, regulators, is it? The Association regulators were having difficulties with the Sioux."

"There's that, too," Ridgeway replied a bit stiffly.

Hastily Rebecca came back. "I didn't mean to offend, or to intrude."

"No offense taken, Sam. The fact is that the off-reservation Sioux are becoming a menace and a hazard. They're hostiles, according to the Army, and lately they've been hindering our operations. There has been a lot of missing cattle, not only from my ranch but from others. A few dead ranch hands. It didn't take long. I remember having to fight to keep my place back when the territory first opened up. I wasn't opposed to doing so again. We, those who are members of the Cattlemen's Association, got together and discussed the problem. Alystaire Carmoody, I believe I've mentioned him before? He's president of the Association, and the one who brought in the regulators. For a while it seemed to help. A few white rustlers caught, some skirmishes with the free Sioux, and our losses declined." Ridgeway's expression changed, scowl lines forming on his high, sun-browned forehead.

"It wasn't until I got too deeply committed that I began to suspect the truth."

"How do you mean that, Grover? What 'truth'?"

"Oh, it's nothing, perhaps. It's only that . . . Carmoody continues to talk about taking over the territory, of splitting it up among the members of the Association and throwing out anyone who objects. Even that had a certain appeal. Lately though, I . . ." Ridgeway let his voice dwindle until they rode a few paces in silence. "Enough of serious talk. That's not what you're interested in, anyway. With everyone back at headquarters by Saturday it's going to be a perfect time for that welcoming party. And I'm sure you'll take to my sons every bit as much as they will to you. Up ahead there, Pine Creek enters the White. We'll ford there and swing east. I want to show you my stone quarry and sawmill. They're the real treasures that made this place possible."

"That sounds fascinating, Grover." What fascinated Rebecca most was this first unplanned revelation of discontent with Carmoody and the hint that some, if not all of the Association's activities might be illegal.

Chapter 16

Lt. Joseph Demarris had taken over command of A Company after Arnulf Larsen's "suicide." The chill gray dawn found him and his men in the field, along with B Company, freshly back from detached duty. A diffused pink glowed on the eastern skyline as the troopers saddled up and made ready for another day in the saddle. The odor of coffee, from their predawn breakfast, lingered in the still, cold air. Joe Demarris wished fervently that he had a cup in his icy hands at that moment.

"Company's saddled and ready to ride, sir," his first sergeant informed him as he approached. "The colonel's compliments, and first platoon is to take the point."

"Very well, Sergeant Thompkins."

Demarris wished that Arnie Larsen was there. They had been friends, close since their days at West Point. He had a strong suspicion regarding the so-called suicide, one he dared not discuss with anyone. On several occasions he had caught Sergeant Thompkins eyeing him closely. What did the sergeant know? As though reading the officer's thoughts, Sergeant Thompkins, instead of walking away to attend to his duties, stepped closer to the officer and spoke in a quiet tone.

"Sir, what do you know about Lieutenant Larsen? About his death, I mean, sir?"

"Why, it's officially been ruled a suicide."

"Beggin your pardon, sir, but that's bullshit, and you know it just as well as I do, sir."

Demarris looked long and hard at this first sergeant. "Exactly what *do* you know, First Sergeant?"

Thompkins came even closer and spoke in a lower voice. "I know it was me who got into the records and sent Mr. Larsen's true report to headquarters on the fight with those Sioux hunters. I'm also fairly sure it was you or Mr. O'Day who made an unauthorized report on the killing of that old Indian the other day."

Demarris caught a gasp before it escaped and he swallowed hard. Thompkins knew too damned much, considering Demarris didn't yet know on whose side the sergeant played. But Thompkins had admitted rifling official files to do a risky thing for a dead man's honor. Joe Demarris bit his lip a moment before making a response.

"Yeah. I did that. And I'm not the least convinced that Arnie, er, Lieutenant Larsen killed himself. Why would he?"

"That's right, sir. I was there, I saw the same things he did. Those Oglala didn't attack us. It was the other way around. And I saw and heard when Colonel Peyton ordered the guard force to fire on an unarmed man. When Clanahan stuck that little boy it made me sick."

Bitterness colored Demarris's words. "The colonel seemed to enjoy it well enough."

"Beggin' your pardon, sir, but the colonel, sir, is an asshole. Clanahan's a bit crazy or he wouldn't have done it. The men in this company will have no truck with him since he bayoneted that kid. But, you've relieved my mind on one matter. Now, sir, if it's not a presumption, sir, I've a favor to ask of you."

"What's that?"

"Would you join with me, sir, and some others to see Mr. Larsen's memory and record are done justice? And to get rid of that madman, Peyton, before he causes another war? Will you, sir?"

"That sounds like mutiny, Sergeant."

"Oh, no, sir. Not in the least, sir. We mean to do it the right and proper way, through channels. Even if one of us has to quit the army, like Mr. Larsen."

"Do you think department headquarters or the Secretary of War would listen to an *ex*-sergeant any more than a former lieutenant?"

"No, sir. We've though that over, me'n the boys who want what's right for Mr. Larsen. They wouldn't listen to just any ol' ex-sergeant, like you say, sir. But they would listen to the new senior vice president of Thompkins Arms Company. You see, sir, it's my father who owns the foundry that provides all those fancy swords for you officers."

"Well I'll be goddamned," Demarris exploded in astonishment. "My dress sword *is* a Thompkins. My father got it for me at graduation from the Point. I never knew that, Sergeant."

"I don't much go in for braggin', sir."

"All right, then, Thompkins, we have an agreement. Only I don't think it will be necessary for anyone to quit the Army in order to make this work."

"I hope you're right, sir."

"We have to keep this absolutely secret. I agree that Colonel Peyton is not in control of all of his faculties. One misstep and we could wind up like poor Arnie."

"Is this what you call a good day's work, Mr. Demarris?" Lt Col. Bryce Peyton demanded when the two troops halted for the evening.

"Well, ah, no, sir. Our point came upon two hostiles and took them prisoner. There was no sign of others. It's my conclusion that they are hunters. Something big must be going on right now. No large parties out, no raids reported. Remember sir, they've lost a chief. There's always a big affair a-doing to elect another one."

"Are you lecturing me on Indians, sir?"

151

"Ah, no, sir. I'd not presume to do that sir. It was merely a reminder. I'm sure you have many things of greater importance to occupy your mind than keeping track of what the savages might be doing."

"Yes. Yes, of course, Mr. Demarris. Nevertheless, I am most disappointed that we callused our behinds for nothing more that a warrior barely out of his teens and a stripling youth. Two birds is better than an empty bag, I suppose. Have them brought to me. I wish to interrogate them before evening chow."

"Yes, sir."

Within five minutes, Demarris and four men returned with the young Sioux captives. The Oglalas glanced about warily and stood shoulder-to-shoulder when brought before the colonel. Demarris could not help but feel sorry for the younger one. He must not be more than fourteen or fifteen. The boy had been roughed up some during his capture and was obviously frightened, though he tried hard not to show it.

"Get Mr. Nasturtium in here," Peyton demanded.

"It's Posey, sir," Demarris supplied. "Willis Posey."

"Posey, Nasturtium, what difference does it make? These civilian scouts are all alike. Indian-lovers the lot, or they wouldn't know that barbarian language."

Posey, in buckskins and smelling of wood smoke, arrived a few minutes later. "Had to finish my victuals, Colonel."

"Like hell you did, Pansy. I want to make myself understood to these vermin. And I want a true and accurate account of what they say."

Posey turned to the Oglalas, greeted them, gave his name, and asked for theirs. "They say they're Black Tail and Spotted Belly, Colonel."

"Are they from that big band of Red Tops?"

No hesitation came after the translation. "Yes. Black Tail, the older one, says they were out makin' meat. That means hunting, colonel."

"Tell them that they're liars and that I know it."

Anger entered the tone of Black Tail's voice. He shook his

head forcefully and tried to sign in the negative with his bound hands. *"Hecitu yelo!"*

"He says he speaks the truth, Colonel."

Colonel Peyton took up a cigar from the bent-over lip of a peach can. He knocked off the ash and drew on it until a thick cherry coal glowed brightly. Then he drove the fiery tip against Black Tail's right breast, burning deeply into flesh. Black Tail writhed but did not cry out.

"Lyin Oglala scum. Tell him I can look into his soul. Tell him I can see a black-hearted liar and coward."

While the translation was being made, Peyton came around his folding camp desk and aimed a solid kick at young Spotted Belly's groin. The boy's testicles crushed agonizingly under the impact of the colonel's boot toe. Spotted Belly fell to the ground sobbing in excruciating pain.

"Colonel," Lt. Demarris injected urgently. "Your pardon, sir, but you had no cause to strike that boy. You had none at all to do what you did."

Peyton chose to ignore his subordinate. "What's going on in your village? How many war parties have been set out?"

" 'None,' " he says. " 'None. Only hunting parties. There is a council to elect the new chief.' "

Black Tail's head still hung and Peyton gave him solid backhand swipes on both cheeks, splitting one lip. "Answer me, you stupid brute!"

"Seems how I r'col'ect he just did, Colonel."

"No impudence from you, Posey!"

"A'right, a'right, tell you what you do, Colonel. You just get yourself a new interpreter, Colonel. 'Cause this ol' son ain't gonna do one fuckin' word more, y'hear? You should know by now these folks don't know how to make up a direct lie. If I thought for a second they was shadin' the truth, I'd have wrung it outta 'em in a flash. You're hearin' the truth, Colonel. Thing is you ain't hearin' what you *want* to hear."

"Don't take one step from this tent, Posey," Peyton thundered.

"I'll do as I see fit, Colonel. I plum up an' quit the Army."

"I'll have you arrested, Posey."

"Now, Colonel, I don't think I'd take kindly to the attempt. The last fellah you arrested wound up hung in his cell."

Bryce Peyton blanched a sickly gray-white and turned away from the spectators in his tent. It took a visible effort of will for him to recover his composure. When he turned around his eyes had gone dark with anger and his voice rang with a sepulchral tone.

"Take these recalcitrant hostiles out and hang them."

"Colonel, you can't!" Demarris shouted.

"I can and I will."

"They've done nothing wrong, there's no charge against them."

"Oh, yes, they have. They're Sioux, aren't they? Oglala Sioux who murdered Custer. That's charge enough."

"You can't even prove they were there."

"I don't need to. You men, do as I say. Report to the sergeant major and make these men ready for execution."

"Colonel, I beg you. . . ."

"*Silence*, Lieutenant. We'll make up the matter of your insubordination later. For now, hold your tongue and see that the sentence is carried out."

Five minutes later, Black Tail and Spotted Belly sat astride bareback horses. Their hands had been securely tied behind them and thick-knotted ropes had been fitted around their necks. Colonel Bryce Peyton supervised personally. He licked his lips with the slow, avid strokes of a man anticipating a sexual encounter. An unnatural quiet held over the camp as he raised his hand for the signal.

When it dropped, the horses were struck on the rump by two burly sergeants and they bolted out from under the helpless Oglala youths. Sickened by the barbaric spectacle, Lieutenant Demarris turned away, seething with bitter, impotent anger.

A whippoorwill sounded its haunting call through the

predawn cold. Pasu Tanka nodded in satisfaction. Everyone would be in position. The time had come. From the direction where the signal had sounded, cattle lowed in the frosty morn, eager for the light and scant warmth that would allow them to feed once more. Big Nose chaffed under the council's decision.

"Do not kill the white men if you can avoid it," he had been told. "Hurt him where it is important. Kill his animals, burn his lodge but spare his life. We must show that we do not want war, only what the whites call justice."

He'd do his best to see that it went like that. If the whites got in the way, though . . . Pasu Tanka knew what to do. Cold-stiffened joints responded slowly as he raised from a crouch and swung onto his favorite war pony.

"It's time," he said softly.

Beside him, a young apprentice struck flint and steel, blew on the sparks that landed in the nest of fine milkweed fuzz and ignited the brand. When it flamed well, he handed it to Big Nose. Grunting his approval, Big Nose watched other torches come to life in a crescent-shaped line. Then he kneed his pony forward and the war party sprang to life.

They swept down toward the darker clumps of buildings and divided their force to different tasks. Those with torches swung toward a tall barn that housed a winter's supply of hay. Beyond it lay the bunkhouse. Others surged in among the vapor-smoking forms of cattle.

Branch Delano and six of his hands became aware of the raid simultaneously. They managed to yank on trousers and shrug into heavy coats while the first wounded cattle still bawled in misery. The defenders snatched up rifles and rushed into the open. The dreaded shapes of Sioux warriors stood out in the moonlight. Winchesters began to spit fire. Then a terrible cry went up.

"The barn! They're firing the barn!"

More cowmen scrambled from the bunkhouse as flames began to crackle on the roof. They fired wildly, more intent on saving the precious hay and their own lodgings than on killing the Sioux.

Big Nose heard a grunt of pain and noted that Red Wolf had been wounded. He steadied his mount sufficiently to take aim and sent a slug into the white man who had fired the harmful shot. The *wasicun* cried out and slammed back against the wall of the burning lodge. More cattle bellowed their agony and the last of the torches flew into the barn. Big Nose raised in his stirrups and let loose a piercing call.

At once the raiders responded to the signal. Swiftly they whirled their horses, and like a wraith of smoke on a windy night, disappeared into nothing. Only their drumming hoofbeats and the roar of flames gave evidence they had ever been there.

"You sons of bitches!" Branch Delano yelled helplessly. "You heathen cowards. Come back and fight!"

Crashing timbers on the haymow answered him.

Chapter 17

Slogging heavily through the brisk cold of morning, the two troops returned to Camp Cullen. The summary hanging of the Oglala youths weighed heavily on everyone except Lieutenant Colonel Peyton. His mood seemed light, compared to recent weeks. Few wanted to comment on it, though, and more than one trooper wondered why he had ever joined the Army. After the men had been formed up on the parade and dismissed, Peyton entered headquarters with a jaunty step.

His pleasure turned to dust when he entered his office and saw the cynical eyes and mocking sneer of Capt. Duncan Stanley. The balding provost marshal rose in a travesty of respect when Peyton entered and stalked to his desk.

"I'm sure you know why I'm here." Stanley came to the point.

"You can't. It's too soon," Peyton blurted in short, broken sentences.

"Oh, come now. We have a working relationship going here. You get money for illegal activities and I share in the wealth to insure silence."

"But, I haven't—haven't been paid any more since . . ."

"You've been getting it right along. I'm only trying to catch up, put things in balance, you see?"

Understanding drew a somber pall over Bryce Peyton.

"You'll never stop, will you? You'll never get *enough*."

Stanley gave him a bleak smile. "You're quite right in those assumptions. I'm your personal leech, attached to you for the rest of your life. But, as I said, I won't be greedy. I only want . . . my share."

"You bastard!" Peyton's expression would have paralyzed a bull buffalo.

"I'm sure by now you have considered killing me as a means of ending our business arrangement. Disabuse yourself of that right now. I've taken the precaution to see that everything I know will immediately be in the hands of higher headquarters in the event of my untimely death. I believe I've brought that up before. But I wanted you to know that I have revised my protection, including the first payment of five hundred you made. Since I don't plan to use the money until my retirement, it's perfectly all right to be enclosed with the summary of your actions and mine. Dead it wouldn't matter a whit to me."

"How can you do something so monstrous?" Peyton said in a strangled voice.

"It's easy. When one has been passed over for promotion as often as I, many things previously unspeakable become expedient."

Peyton bowed to the inevitable. "How much do you want this time?"

"The same. Five hundred dollars."

"But I . . . You'll wipe me out! I—I have expenses. . . ."

"Restrain your extravagances, then. Five hundred, within two days, or I take my story directly to the department commander."

After Stanley's departure, Peyton slumped in his chair, face drawn and haggard. The specter of his precipitous execution of the Oglalas came back to taunt him. Perhaps he should not have done it. If word got back to department headquarters that neither of them had been painted for war . . . Bryce Peyton shuddered and turned his thoughts to his immediate difficulty.

He had so limited a number of choices. He could take the

chance that Duncan Stanley lied and kill the blackmailing captain. Or he could refuse to pay and contrive some sort of counterclaim to confuse the issue and discredit Stanley. He could keep on paying, which was unthinkable. Or . . . his mind rebelled at the prospect . . . he could take his own life.

For what? his calmer self countered. He'd entered into this conspiracy with Alystaire Carmoody and the Association ranchers in order to do the same thing Stanley sought to do. To enhance his fortunes. If he were to end it by his own hand, that would all be for naught. What could he do? What? With all the effort of his will he strove to convince himself there had to be a way.

Laughter rose to the velvety vault studded with stars. The strains of waltzes, mazurkas, and gavottes sweetened the air around the brightly lighted mansion that served as headquarters for Grover Ridgeway's ranch. Ladies in swaying ball gowns pecked daintily at a large array of canapes and sweets created by the redoubtable Mrs. Stout. Hearty laughter came from the men who were enjoying drinks and cigars on the veranda prior to the late dinner that would make welcome the belle of the South, Samantha Waterhouse.

Rebecca Caldwell, in her guise as Samantha Waterhouse, wore a spectacular dress that swayed like a giant elm with each movement. She met each of the influential members of the Cattlemen's Association, their wives, and many other guests. It all seemed so splendid and civilized. In less than half an hour her discomfort at the pretense had dissolved away. Rebecca actually found herself having fun.

"You'll probably not remember five names from among this throng," Grover Ridgeway remarked at her side. "But at least you'll know you are an honored and sought-after guest. Three people have already left invitation cards in the tray on the hall table. You're making quite a hit with these socially starved folks."

"I hope I won't prove a disappointment to them," Rebecca answered sincerely.

"Why, how could you?" Ridgeway paused to replace their empty glasses with more champagne. "Your radiant appearance has brought a sparkle to this house that has too long been absent. Oh-ho, here come my proud progeny. If you doubt me, watch their reaction," he added confidently.

"Hello, Father," a blond, curly-haired youth of fourteen greeted him.

"Good evening, sir," his smaller tow headed brother added.

"Boys, I want you to meet the object of all this gaiety. This is Miss Samantha Waterhouse. Samantha, my sons, Peter and Joey."

In the next instant, Peter, the elder, underwent an amazing transformation. To assign the term lust to the affection of a male child for an older woman, not a relative, would impugn the innocence of childhood. Yet, for Peter the infatuation that radiated from his youthful face came close to it, or better still, utter adoration.

His jaw sagged, his gaze fixed on Rebecca's heart-shaped face, while his pulse rate increased and his eyes glazed. He suddenly flushed a bright pink, assumed a cross-legged posture, and held his head low, hands folded in front of him. Beside Peter, his brother took on the expression of a small babe with a beloved kitten in his arms. Their father, it semed, took no notice of it.

"I see from your cheeks and ears that you managed to remember where-all to scrub for once. Put up your hats and join us for dinner."

"Ah-er, yes, sir," Peter responded in a low tone that squeaked upward with each syllable.

Grover had not missed the dramatic change, Rebecca discovered when the boys made off to hang up their hats and coats. "Didn't I tell you they'd react much the same as I? I think Peter's smitten."

"Grover!" she began, then broke out in a warm chuckle.

"Poor Peter seemed to have something difficult come up all of a sudden. Oh, mercy me, that was hardly a ladylike observation. You'll excuse me, of course."

"Certainly, Sam. Your introduction certainly wasn't intended to make things hard for him," he added with a straight face.

"If I didn't know better, Grover, I'd . . . but no, one gentleman in the world who makes off-color puns is enough. It couldn't be."

"Who might the other be?" Grover Ridgeway responded with no attempt at denial.

"A young man I met in California. Mike Alvarado. He seemed absolutely addicted to them."

"I can see where that could become embarrassing. I'm afraid that around here, without a woman's influence for so many years, the boys have grown up in a rather more frank, open atmosphere than most children. Our personal family humor tends to be rather of the raw and masculine variety. I hope you're not offended."

"Not at all. To the contrary, I'm . . . stimulated by the thought."

Not lacking in perceptivity, Grover Ridgeway gave her a long, speculative look. His evaluation ended with the sound of an adenoidal voice.

"Excuse me, Dad, I have to talk to you about something." Peter Ridgeway had returned.

"What is it, son?" Grover inquired, turning partly away from Rebecca.

"Well, sir," Peter began miserably, "I have this stiff proposition to consider, and . . ."

Grover Ridgeway glanced over his shoulder and winked at Rebecca. Then he put an arm around his son's shoulder and guided him toward the table where drinks were being dispensed. Rebecca stifled a giggle in her lace handkerchief.

"Miss Samantha, may I have the honor of a dance before dinner?"

Rebecca looked down at the mop of white hair in disarray on Joey Ridgeway's head. Small for his age, Joey exhibited a maturity and tact shared by few, if any, twelve-year-olds. Touched, she nodded gravely.

"It is I who would be honored, Joey. Lead the way."

Dinner over, the quartet silent at last, the guests trundled off to bed or home, Rebecca and Grover shared a nightcap in the disorder left behind by the party. Ridgeway lifted his glass in a silent salute.

"It all seems so sad, after the party has ended."

"Oh, I don't know," Rebecca responded. "In a way it's a testimonial to how much fun everyone had. This has been so nice, Grover. Thank you."

Rebecca stood on tiptoe and kissed him lightly on the lips. The explosive emotional shock that both experienced left them momentarily frozen. Then Grover set aside his brandy glass and took her tightly in his arms. His lips turned to lambent flames flickering on hers, while an exquisite pain burst within her breast. Her arms entwined about his neck and her glass shattered on the floor. Heat and hunger radiated from his solid masculine frame. Matching it with an urgency of her own, Rebecca ground her pelvis against him and felt the stirring arousal of his manhood. How long had it remained dormant? she wondered.

"This is—hardly the place," Rebecca panted, her eyes as knowing as his.

"My room, then."

"What about the boys? Your guests?"

"They'll never know. I'm on the far side of the house. Come with me, now."

"I-I can't possibly say no. Oh, Grover . . ."

Together they slipped stealthily down the hall and entered the large master bedroom. The covers had been turned back and the pillows fluffed. Grover took Rebecca in his arms again

162

and kissed her with even more zeal. When the embrace ended, he began to undress. Rebecca did likewise.

"I don't want you to think . . . I mean . . . something, I don't know what, happened tonight. I—I'm not in the habit of sweeping my guests off their feet like . . ."

Rebecca placed warm, moist fingers across his mouth. "Don't say anything. Now's a time for great deeds, not words."

To Rebecca's delight, Grover turned out to have better than average endowments. Her resolve had slipped entirely, her mission forgotten in a sea of champagne, whirling dances, and the gentle touch of his hands.

Grover caressed her again now, more ardently, but no less intimately in feeling than before. No cloth intervened this time and the elctric shock of their contact set Rebecca to trembling.

"Are you cold?"

"No. Just the thought of being with you now is sending shivers down my spine."

Totally aroused himself, Grover needed no further words to urge him on.

His hands moved against her firm breasts, stroking her nipples until she begged him to wait no longer. Rebecca reached out for him then and guided him to her silken flesh. He trembled slightly and a soft moan built in his throat. Rebecca began showering him with kisses.

She reached the hollow of his throat and he gasped harshly. His strong arms swung her off her feet and he carried her to the big bed. Gently he lowered her, then knelt between her upraised knees.

Grover's lips were like cool flames setting her blood on fire. Rebecca arched her back and her small fists pounded the pillow. Dizziness engulfed her and she felt her soul whirling away.

Grover cried out and began a slow rocking. Straining, his body on the verge of going out of control, Grover at last achieved complete satisfaction. Shaking with the pounding of his emotions, he covered her mouth with his and began a long,

163

languid rhythm that slid them both blissfully off into another universe.

"First," Grover gasped out.

"What?"

"Y-you're the first since Cynthia."

Touched by such an expression of faithfulness, Rebecca could not but wonder how such a man could be connected to something evil. For a long moment, guilt burned within her for the deception she was playing. Then her natural, healthy body began to quicken with renewed desire.

"If you're worried about maybe forgetting what to do, you needn't. If you think I might disappear into smoke, be assured I'll be right here. We have a whole, happy night ahead of us."

"Yes. Oh, yes. I never knew how badly I . . . needed someone."

"Then come to me, my love."

Eagerly, Grover Ridgeway complied.

Chapter 18

Angry at the restrictions placed on them by the council, Raven, Laughing Boy, Three Horses, and Eagle Spared Him left the big camp on the Little White River with Two Bulls. Now they and seven followers set off on a raid of their own, sanctioned by Two Bulls. It was the day after Big Nose returned from burning the Delano ranch. They would bring their own kind of war to the whites, Raven had told his small war party. On the morning following Rebecca's welcoming party at the Slash-R-Bar, they found the ideal place to begin.

"Watch them," Raven commanded. "The *wašicun* man feeds his horses. How many others are there?"

"Two," Three Horses responded. "The boy with the white birds, and there is smoke from the wood lodge, a woman cooking." His nose wrinkled at the faint, but obvious scent of frying meat.

"There are more," Raven contradicted him. "See, the clothes drying. I count three sizes of leg coverings. There's another boy somewhere. And the white squares. I have seen white women use those on babies."

Eagle Spared Him grunted agreement. "Where's this other boy? How big is he?"

"Big enough to use a gun. I say he's in the animal lodge," Raven informed them.

165

"Kill the man first," Laughing Boy suggested.

"Yes," Raven agreed. "The man and the two boys. Šunktanka-yam'ni, take one hand of the men and circle around. I'll stay here and lead the rest against the house. If we strike all at once there can be no way to stop us. The whites will be confused, frightened. They'll fall easily."

The treeless, gently rolling prairie west of the White River provided little concealment, yet the Oglala warriors disappeared into the terrain in fleeting moments. Three Horses led his contingent in a wide circle around the farmstead and made ready for the attack.

Tom Ellis looked up at the sound of rapid, pounding hoofbeats. Across the flat pasture north of the barn streamed six Sioux warriors. Their yips and war cries shattered the morning stillness. Tom darted toward the granary to recover his rifle while he yelled a warning to his family.

"Indians! Homer, stay in the barn, lock it up. Esther, stay in the house. Close the shutters."

His younger son, Evan, dropped the battered pot from which he scattered feed for the chickens. Head down, he ran toward his father, on a course that would intersect his parent's outside the grain storage shed. A rifle crashed a short distance away and Evan looked up to see his father jolted forward. The elder Ellis made the last three paces to the low building and fell partly inside, across the threshold.

"Daddy!" Evan screamed as he pumped his legs faster.

Evan came closer and saw a red stain spreading over his father's back. His momentum sent him sprawling when he tried to halt. Tom Ellis looked up at his son, blood running from his mouth.

"My rifle. Get my rifle and close yourself in the granary."

"But, Daddy . . ."

"Do it. I'm killed, Evan. Drag me out and shut the door behind you."

Tears blurred Evan's vision. For a moment he hesitated.

"*Do it!*" his father shouted in a frightening voice.

166

Evan bent to obey as an arrow snapped past, through the area where his chest had been a moment before. How heavy his father seemed. His tears flowed freely now and he sobbed in grief and desperation. Once more he heaved. Tom Ellis helped all he could. The slightly-built boy managed to tumble his father's body out of the doorway. Quickly he came upright and yanked the door toward him.

Not fast enough. An arrow quivered in his skinny chest, and a fifty-six-caliber bullet shattered his skull in the fraction of a second he remained exposed. Driven backward, the dead boy fell over a stack of grain sacks. The Ellis horses whinnied in fright, and gunshots came from the haymow.

"The grass lodge," Three Horses shouted. "Make fire in the grass lodge."

Dust obscured the farmyard. A piercing shriek came from the house. Glistening with sweat and oil, two braves swung a fence post in a furious attempt to smash down the door. Homer took careful aim and fired from the haymow door. His bullet entered the small of Eagle Helps Him's back and shattered the Oglala's spine.

Upper body rigid, legs pumping uncontrollably, Eagle Helps Him drove himself face-first into the door and fell backward. Paralyzed from the waist down, but not dead, he howled in agony. Homer smelled smoke and heard flames crackling from below. More Indians swarmed outside. He had to ignore it, the black-haired boy told himself. He had to help his mother and little sister. He shouldered the Winchester and fired again.

Wood splintered beside Fat Otter's face. He winced at the tiny needles of pain the slivers caused and swung the improvised ram once more. Beyond the stout panel he heard a cracking sound.

"Once more," Fat Otter told his companions.

They swung the ram as Homer Ellis fired again. The door gave way with a bang and three Oglalas entered in a rush. A fourth joined Eagle Helps Him, writhing in agony on the porch. Screams rose from inside. Then a single shot. Homer began to cry as the warriors dragged his mother's lifeless form from the house. Mechanically he chambered another round and fired at the Sioux below. His sight picture obscured by tears, he sent a slug into the forehead of a prancing pony. It dropped instantly to the ground, pinning its rider with a lifeless flank. More flames rose up. Homer knew he hadn't long to live.

Regret rose in his thirteen-year-old breast. He fought it down with the determination to take as many Indians along with him as he could.

Two more Šayaota Oglala died before heat and smoke drove Homer into the open. Half a dozen bullets riddled his slender frame and Homer Ellis dropped in heap. Silently, with a solemn face, Raven dismounted and took the boy's scalp.

"He fought bravely and died a man. We will honor him in our victory dance," he informed the others.

Dappled sunlight filtered through the burlap curtains of the line shack. Since shortly after the midday meal, Rebecca Caldwell and Grover Ridgeway had been riding the open plains of his vast ranch. They had shotguns along and sought to bag enough quail for a small dinner that evening. Both of Grover's sons had been disappointed when they had not been included in the expedition. That was to be expected. Now, as Rebecca stretched luxuriously on the narrow bunk, she felt not the least regret at leaving the youngsters behind.

"You make marvelous love in the afternoon, Grover," she told him sincerely. "Law, among my set back home the very idea is scandalous. That seems to add a sort of savor to it all."

"You've awakened emotions and desires in me that I'd long ago forgotten existed, Sam," her lover replied in all honesty. "I can't deny that I've been lonely. Some of the time without knowing it. My boys have suffered most, I suppose. They needed a mother. Still do, for that matter."

Grover paused, as though astounded at the words he had let escape. Rebecca used the opportunity to examine her dreadfully mixed emotions regarding this handsome, consummate lover, whom she also believed to be capable of unconscionable crimes. Nothing seemed to fit right.

A widower, who loved his two children, adored his housekeeper, and had a quick mind didn't fit her concept of a monster. His words of only a moment before spoke of hunger, loss, and compassion. Of a sudden she didn't want to find anything that tied him to the Carmoody cabal. All she wanted was his arms around her, his powerful body embracing her own. She reached out, and caressed his muscular flesh.

"If I didn't know better, I'd suspect those sweet words were intended as a preamble to a proposal. Though I don't worry so much about the boys' loneliness as I do about yours. *That* we can do something about right now."

And, oh, yes, oooh, so wonderfully, they did.

On the ride back to the ranch, hours later, Ridgeway brought up the subject again. "Being a widower becomes habit after a while," he observed, as though speaking for his own benefit. "The longer you go, the less the ache of your initial loss and the less your desire for anyone new to replace the missing loved one. One would think it would be the opposite, that the grief early on would get in the way of, ah, that sort of thing. Oh, the boys would wake up crying for Cynthia—they were only three and five when she died of a fever—during the first few years, but with the passage of time, at least for me, it became . . ." he shrugged, "the way things were. But now . . . forgive me, Sam. I'm putting you in a terrible position. Saying too much, as it were, too soon. Tomorrow I'll be busy with ranch business. Why don't you make free to seek anything that interests you. Maybe take Peter and Joey with you. Get to know them a little better."

"I'm grateful, Grover, and . . . I'm touched. With Peter's crush on me, what would such an excursion accomplish, I wonder?"

Ridgeway smiled. "If everything goes as I wish, it won't do any harm to increase Peter's affection for you. Give it a try," he pleaded. "Let yourself, ah, expand here. Learn more about the place and its people."

"How could I refuse?"

Black anger met them at the ranch house. Branch Delano and his wife, with seven of his hands, waited under the widespread shade of a cottonwood. Tables had been set out and the travelers were partaking of refreshments when Rebecca and Grover trotted up to the tie-rail.

"About time you got back here," Delano growled.

"Here we've been nearly murdered in our beds and you go off on a pleasure jaunt with never a thought for others." Edyth Delano, a bitter, petty woman with the overbearing personality of the self-righteous, rose with effort and snapped her words from under eyes that glittered malevolently at Rebecca

Real concern showed in Grover Ridgeway's expression. "Branch, Edyth, what's happened?"

"As if you didn't know," the crippled wife of Branch Delano shot back nastily. "I've had to live with being maimed once by those hideous savages. To endure another assault by them is monstrous."

"We, ah, we had a raid over on my spread, Grover," Branch Delano injected, casting his wife a dark look.

"Raid, is it?" Edyth Delano cawed. "The Sioux, *Mister* Ridgeway, killed our horses and cattle, run off what they didn't slaughter, burned our barn, wounded some of the men. It's a wonder we were spared at all."

"It's not as bad as all that, my dear," Delano added in an attempt to mollify his wife. "We drove them off before they came anywhere near the house."

"When did this happen?" the astonished Grover Ridgeway inquired.

"Three days ago."

"Why is it *your* place was spared?" Edyth asked, with her usual suspicion.

170

Grover ignored her. "How bad, Branch?"

"Nobody killed, at least. Three hands wounded slightly. I lost all my winter hay. Maybe ten horses, forty or fifty cows run off. Twenty of my herd were killed outright."

"What can I do to help?"

"I want you to come with me to see Carmoody. Then the three of us can take it to the Army at Camp Cullen. Carmoody's friend Peyton should be able to make quite a case with this news."

A fleeting frown shaded Grover's brow. "I'm sure he can. I don't know, Branch, I'm mighty busy right at this time. You don't really need me. Alystaire will do all he can for you, I'm confident of that."

"What did I tell you, Mr. Delano?" Edyth Delano injected in a sour tone. "*He* wouldn't lift a finger if we'd all been massacred."

"Edyth, you forget yourself," Branch cautioned mildly.

"It's not *I* who forget myself. Husband, you gave your word we would not have any danger from savages. Elsewise I would never have consented to moving to this forsaken country. Look at him smirking at me while he shows off his *fancy girl.*"

"Edyth!" Delano exploded in shock and embarrassment.

"You're obviously not feeling well, Edyth," Ridgeway began.

"No, Grover, let me speak for myself," Rebecca said quietly. "Mrs. Delano, where I come from, ladies do not inject themselves into the business of gentlemen. Also, women of every class learn early to mind their manners. Obviously, your Yankee upbringing has spared you these important niceties of civilized living."

"Well said, Sam," Grover Ridgeway verbally applauded her.

"You'll not go with me to see Carmoody, then?" Branch Delano asked icily.

"Of course I will, Branch. It's the least I can do. We can't leave before tomorrow, however. Let's go inside, freshen up, and then we can discuss how we're going to present this to

171

Colonel Peyton."

Trapped by her rash statement of a moment ago, Rebecca could say nothing. She withheld her opinion until she again had Grover alone in the large parlor, waiting for the Delanos to join them.

"Grover, after what you said the other day, do you think it's right to press for the Army to go against these Indians?"

"I . . . no. I don't feel right about it. Yet, Branch is a friend. One of long standing. He's been victimized by this thing of Carmoody's, like I have."

"Like the Sioux?"

"Uh . . . yes, like the Sioux, as well. Even so, I can't turn my back now. We might be playing into Alystaire's hands this way, but Branch has suffered a terrible loss, and someone must be made to pay."

"It's all so confusing," Rebecca injected to keep her cover intact. "I declare, I could never figure it all out."

"I have a hard enough time doing so and . . . on more than one occasion I've come to regret my decision."

"Then follow your feelings now. That's what I would do."

"I should. I can't, though. I'd be letting down a man who trusts me and needs my help. Bryce Peyton is a man consumed with hatred for the Indians. Carmoody has hardly less aversion to them. You've seen the effect Edyth Delano's enmity has on her husband. The three of them, together, could precipitate a disaster. Perhaps by being along, I can moderate the situation."

"You spoke today as though you wanted to make a break with these men. Why not do it now?"

Grover took Rebecca by the shoulders and drew her close. "I want to, I know I must. Something inside, though, tells me now is not the time. I'll go. And afterward, we can plan together how I can extricate myself from this entire mess."

"I'll miss you while you're gone."

A rueful expression formed on Ridgeway's handsome face. "You could try praying for me. I think I might need it."

Chapter 19

Thick white bands of cigar smoke swayed lazily in the office of Lieutenant Colonel Bryce Peyton. His three civilian visitors had indeed brought him good news. Not that the burning of the Delano place was good, of course, but it was a reason, the excuse, at last, to mount a major expedition against the hostile Sioux. He positively beamed at them when their presentation ended.

"I have all six companies back in garrison now. This couldn't have come at a better time."

Branch Delano scowled at this remark. "Now just a minute, Colonel. . . ."

"Tut! I didn't mean that in the way you took it, Mr. Delano, for I deeply regret the loss of your property. Rather that now is the only time in the past four months when I, ah, the Army could do something effective. My companies are understrength as it is. Without all of them there would be no way to exterminate these renegades. I'll see that orders for the field are initiated at once. We should be on the march within three days." When he saw Alystaire Carmoody's reaction, he hastened to add, "Some of the troops need reoutfitting and all furloughs will have to be cancelled. Then there's the ammunition wagons, food for the men and fodder for the horses, the artillery to make ready. All of those things take time."

Peyton paused, eyes alight with eagerness. He rubbed his hands together and reached for a steel nib pen.

"If you can give me the details. Enemy strength and location, that sort of thing, it will help a great deal."

"I haven't any information along those lines," Grover Ridgeway offered as he rose from his chair. "If you'll excuse me, Colonel?"

"Oh, ah, yes. Quite all right, Mr. Ridgeway." After Ridgeway's departure, Peyton asked conspiratorially, "What about him? He seemed rather unenthusiastic about this campaign. After all, it's what we've all wanted, isn't it?"

"I'm a bit worried myself," Carmoody responded. "You heard what Grover had to say earlier about driving the Sioux onto reservations, not eliminating them. He's mellowed a lot since those first hands of his were, ah, 'killed by the Sioux.'"

Bryce Peyton winced at the mention of the murders. Although not directly involved, he had been responsible for investigating and making a determination. His most cursory review of the facts made it clear that white men had been responsible, in fact he had identified the perpetrators as three of the Cattlemen's Association Range Detectives. Yet he had carefully tailored his report to suggest that it had been renegade Oglalas who had slain the men. Initially it had won Grover Ridgeway over to the grand plan that Alystaire Carmoody and he himself had devised. What could have shaken Ridgeway's loyalty?

"Why has Ridgeway become disaffected with the plan?" the colonel inquired.

"He has a new lady-love in his life," Branch Delano answered with a sour note.

Aware of the bitter, rarely sweet, relationship between Branch Delano and his wife, Peyton could not suppress the flicker of a smile. "Oh! I see. That could certainly account for a lot of things. But such infatuations are relatively short-lived, eh? The reality rarely measures up to the expectation. I think our Mr. Ridgeway will come around, given enough time."

Out on the porch of the headquarters building, Grover Ridgeway stood with his hands behind his back, staring off across the parade ground. His stomach boiled every bit as much as his emotions. Cannon to use against women and children? He considered the very suggestion barbaric. His own arguments for pushing the Sioux onto the reservations had been totally ignored.

"It's too late for that," Colonel Peyton had snapped. "Save for the few who are running with the wild Cheyenne out to the west, these are the last of those responsible for the Custer massacre. The time's overdue that they be taught a lesson."

So absolute, so assured—yet the words rang in Grover's head with a terrible note of insincerity. For the hundredth time he wished he hadn't come. Had his mere presence sealed the fate of the Oglala? Misery washed at the edges of his conscience like a persistent surf. The door opened behind him and his fellow civilians came out.

"Well, that's all settled," Carmoody announced, rubbing his hands together in satisfaction.

More like Pilate washing his hands in front of Christ, Grover thought. Carmoody continued his gloating recitation.

"Peyton couldn't be happier. Now he has his excuse to get the revenge he's been dreaming of since his son was killed by the Cheyenne and Custer got it at the Big Horn. There's going to be a lot of dead Sioux laying around. You can count on that. I've volunteered half of the regulators to ride with the army. The rest I'm going to put to driving out the last of the Nesters. Buck up there, Grover. Within sixty days, we'll have claim to all the land from Minnesota to the Bad Lands."

"It's nice of you to show me around, Peter," Rebecca Caldwell told Grover Ridgeway's older son.

"I'd do anything for you, Miss Samantha," Peter replied in a worshipful voice.

Like the jab of a hat pin, guilt stabbed her painfully. What had begun as a convenience had turned into a barrier.

Her pretense prevented any true show of her feelings. She found Peter and Joey to be charming, their sweet innocence rough-edged just enough to make them healthy, normal boys. Now she hated her dishonesty in living a false life. Because, and her heart ached with the admission, she found herself falling in love with their father.

Grover Ridgeway. Could a man be more mismatched within himself than he? Why had he gone with Delano? Rebecca had read the anguish of indecision on Grover's face when he had firmly stated his intention of making the trip to see Carmoody and then on to Camp Cullen. Less than half an hour later he had expressed his doubts about Carmoody. He'd admitted he wanted no part of killing women and children. Had he prevailed? Had he managed to moderate the demands for severe "punishment" for the Oglala?

Considering what she knew of Lieutenant Colonel Bryce Peyton, Rebecca feared greatly that he had not. Somehow Two Bulls and the Sayaota had to be warned. Worse, she had to play out her charade and look for incriminating evidence. A lead fist closed over her heart at the prospect of finding any.

"What was that?" she asked, suddenly aware that Peter had directed a question to her.

"I asked if you wanted to see the cattle we brought in to winter pasture."

"Oh, yes. That would be nice."

"You're thinkin' about Dad, right?" Peter asked with a grin.

"Uh, yes, Peter." Though not the way you think, she added mentally.

"I sort of miss him, too. He doesn't go away for more'n a day, usually. Even when we're out on the range, away from him, I always know he's close by. I,uh, don't like that Mr. Delano," he confided suddenly. "Do you?"

176

"Now that you mention it, Peter, no. I don't think much at all of him."

Peter grinned broadly, a little boy sharing confidences. They rode on in silence for a while, topping a rise close to the ranch headquarters. A valley, with high bluffs to the north and east, spread below them. In the deep depression formed there, hundreds of cattle grazed. Rebecca quickly noticed the most distinguishing feature. None of them had the wide, dangerous rack of horns of the typical Texas strain. Their wooly brown sides had already thickened for winter and their compact, sturdy bodies looked eminantly capable of withstanding the terrible cold of the northern prairie in January and February.

"They're beautiful," she enthused.

"Dad's mighty proud of them," Peter responded.

"He should be. Their hair's so thick," Rebecca observed.

"These are the three-year-olds. Most of them were dropped by cows that had been here three to five years. The original stock's more used to cold than Texas cows because they come from country where there's long winters."

"You're quite a stockman yourself, Peter," Rebecca replied sincerely, impressed with the boy's knowledge and casual manner.

Young Ridgeway blushed. Eyes cut away from direct contact, he replied in a low voice. "Awh, it's nothin', really. You learn that sort of stuff workin' with cattle. It's gettin' close to noonin'. I'll race you to the windbreak."

Peter referred to a line of healthy junipers that had been planted between the corrals and the pasture. Enjoying the challenge, Rebecca readily agreed. They set off with wild whoops.

Peter won by a length and a half, although he tried mightily to check rein his mount and let Rebecca forge ahead. Their laughter rebounded from the outbuildings as they trotted to the corral. Joey, who had been working with the hostler all morning, repairing harnesses, joined them there.

"I'm hungry enough to eat a saddle," he chirped. "Where do we eat?"

"At the big house, stupid," his brother told him shortly.

"They're havin' son of a bitch stew at the cookshack," Joey answered defensively.

"Some other time, kid," Peter informed him.

Mrs. Stout had outdone herself. The boys' eyes grew round at the sight of a steaming platter of corned beef and tongue, bowls of potatoes, corn and cabbage, and huge cream puffs for desert. Rebecca reflected with concern that if she ate here for long she would founder. Hearty eaters, though slender in build, the boys set to with knife and fork in hand.

"I'm going to rest for a while," Rebecca announced as she pushed back from the table. "Then, Joey, you can show me your handiwork of this morning."

Joey swelled with pride. "You really wanna see it?"

"Of course."

"It ain't, er, isn't much," he depreciated, correcting his grammar automatically.

"All the same, you did it."

"When do you want to go?"

"In an hour or so."

The boys departed to their own pursuits, which, with Mrs. Stout busy in the kitchen, left Rebecca free to roam the house. She strolled from room to room in a casual manner, working her way to Grover Ridgeway's small office and study. Once there, she closed the door tightly behind her and went directly to his desk. She fervently hoped she would find nothing to directly tie Ridgeway to any criminal activity. Her heart nearly stopping, she opened the first drawer.

Account books and ledgers for the ranch operation filled it. Those she would save for later. Rebecca slid out another compartment. The contents appeared to be correspondence. Dreading what she might discover, she lifted out the carefully made pile and scanned the top one.

After the usual greeting and comments about the weather

178

and the health of the recipient, the text turned serious. "The greatest problem we're going to have to face is not the Sioux, but these sodbusting vermin who are moving in like a plague of locust. The Army will do nothing to them, so it will have to be up to us. That's why I want to take on more regulators for the Association. To do that, I'll need your vote."

The missive went on in that vein for another two paragraphs and was signed, "A. Carmoody." Rebecca's heart felt heavy. Although the letter didn't show a commitment on Grover's part to anything against the law, it had strong implications. She looked at another.

Carmoody again. "Even though you said you didn't want it, I'm sending along your share from those 'stolen' cattle we rounded up from those vermin west of the White. You'd better go ahead and take it, Grover, or the others might become suspicious of your loyalty." The damning paragraph came midway in the letter and went on to say, "The regulators are doing a good job. So far seven rustlers apprehended—seven rustlers hanged. A mighty good score, I'd say."

Reading the words, Rebecca felt sick. The third epistle started off with the chilling words, "We've about set the mood for a 'big game hunt.' Nothing could have helped more than that train's being attacked. I can see Peyton's face when we report all the terrible things the Sioux have been doing. He's going to love having the chance to hunt down the last of the hostiles and dragging the remnants of the once-frightening Sioux to the reservation. Peyton will be after them like a pride of lions."

Apalled, Rebecca sat staring at the three sheets of paper. How could anyone countenence such a horrid scheme? She tried to visualize Grover Ridgeway's being delighted by this information. Somehow she could not. Slowly, one dim flicker of hope emerged.

According to the dates, all of these letters had been sent during the three weeks prior to her arrival at the ranch. The cold, feral joy that communicated itself in the author's words could well be the reason for Grover's recent disaffection with his associates.

It had to be. She could hope for nothing else. Yet the fact remained that this terrible plan had now been set in motion. She had to get word to the Oglala, even if that meant her going herself.

Chapter 20

Only a zealous rooster broke the silence of the frigid dawn. A kerosene lamp in the cookhouse flung a yellow shaft on the frost-covered ground. Smoke rose lazily from the stack. Only the cook and his helpers had stirred out of the bunkhouse. Rebecca Caldwell moved like a silent wraith from the main house to the stable. She had with her the damning letters taken from Ridgeway's office. At best, she hoped to convince Deputy Marshal Philo Bates that Alystaire Carmoody was engineering the Indian trouble and that Grover Ridgeway had disassociated himself from the plot.

Perhaps that way, something could be salvaged. Her heart ached over the necessary betrayal of Peter and Joey. The boys would see it no other way. And their father? If only . . . somehow . . . she could manage to clear his name and keep him out of prison, then someday, maybe, he would understand and forgive. So intent was she on expiating her guilt that she started violently when a horse snorted close beside her.

"There, there," she murmured as she reached out and patted its velvety nose.

Quickly Rebecca located the horse she had been riding each day, slipped the bridle over its muzzle, and positioned the bit. She walked it from the stall and saddled it in dim starlight. A thin ribbon of white lay along the eastern horizon when she left the rear door of the stable and crossed the corral. The protests of awakening men came from the bunkhouse. With a deft movement Rebecca opened the gate and passed through. The wooden rails back in place, she started off, walking her mount away from the headquarters. She had reached the line of junipers when a small, sorrow-filled voice, heavy with accusation, halted her.

"You're runnin' away."

Standing among the dark green boughs, Joey Ridgeway faced her, bare arms crossed over his naked chest, clad only in longjohn bottoms and boots. Big tears shone in his eyes and he worked his throat to keep from letting them spill over. As Rebecca stepped nearer, he shivered violently in the cold. Touched to the pit of her grief-labored heart, Rebecca reached out to him.

"Oh, Joey, I have to."

"No, you don't," he cried out miserably.

"But, I do. It's the best for everyone."

"It's not. Why are you doing this? Why?"

Rebecca folded him into her arms and he let the scalding moisture flow from his eyes. His thin shoulders shook from cold and hurt. Rebecca pressed him tightly to her.

"Joey, Joey, there's something . . . I mean, I didn't come here honestly. I'm not Samantha Waterhouse . . . my name's Rebecca Caldwell and I'm half Sioux."

"I don't care," Joey burst out wretchedly. "You're the most beautiful woman in the world an' Petey an' me want you for our mother. Daddy wants you and so do we. Please, please, don't go away."

Anguish pierced her, so that Rebecca had to swallow hard to be able to speak. "Joey, that's something your father and I have to work out. And right now there isn't time. There are some terrible things going to happen soon. Someone has to warn the Oglala that they're being set up for a massacre."

"What?" Joey stiffened.

"No, your father isn't responsible. But I learned of it here

182

and I have to warn them and to try to get the Army stopped."

"I can go. I can tell them. Just—please don't leave."

"I have to, Joey. I can speak their language. I—I came here to bring peace between the ranchers and the Sioux. I *have* to do this, no one else could."

Joey's sobs lessened. "Let me'n Petey go. We could do it."

"No, son. You are a wonderful boy and I've come to love you. Really I have. But, Joey, the Oglala are angry. Some among them want war. Two white boys alone would be too much temptation. I have to be the one. And then, when it's over, I'll be back."

"No you won't," Joey blubbered. "You'll go away an' I'll never have a mom."

Hauntingly, Rebecca recalled Grover's words. *"They were only three and five when Cynthia died."* How desperately Joey must have missed a mother. Helpless for once in a long while, Rebecca struggled to produce a satisfactory answer.

"I—I've left all my clothes here. And a note for your father. I wouldn't go off and not come back after that."

"I know. I heard you moving around in the house, I read the note after you left. It said good-bye to Dad. That's why I came out here."

"You're resourceful, I'll give you that," Rebecca replied, stroking the child's soft white hair. "Did you also read that I said I loved him?"

"Uh-huh. So I knew—I knew you didn't really want to go away."

"Aaah, Joey! If only life could be as simple as it looks seen by a child."

"I'm not a child!" Joey returned hotly. "I'm near growed up."

"All right. For a boy 'near growed up', you must understand that problems aren't always so simple to solve as they might appear. Men your father knows are bound to be hurt by this. Because of that, and the urgency required to prevent any more bloodshed, I can't sit by and do nothing. And, because I am

183

doing something, your father might come to hate me for a while. For deceiving him and taking advantage of his hospitality."

"D'you mean Mr. Delano and Mr. Carmoody? Well, to hell with them. I don't like 'em anyway."

"I don't, either. That's why I must complete my mission." She patted Joey's head once again and held him at arm's length. "Now, you get along back to the house before you freeze."

Although he still rubbed a fading tear from the corner of one eye, Joey smiled. "You'll be back? Promise, Miss Samantha—ah, Rebecca."

"I'll come back, Joey, I promise."

"Please, *please* do. It'll be so lonely with you gone."

Rebecca waited on a low ridge until Joey's short, slight silhouette merged with the shadows at the front of the main house. His terrible loneliness and genuine love ate at her and she wanted to cry like she hadn't done since her first days of captivity in Iron Calf's camp. Battling her heartbreak and shame, she made good time toward the main road. She could travel faster that way, until she had to cut cross-country to the Sayaota encampment.

When she was fifty yards from the entrance to the Ridgeway ranch, four men appeared suddenly, astride their vapor-snorting horses. Rebecca reined in. From this distance she recognized none of them. Walking her mount, she came closer. Not one appeared to be a hand for the /R—. The closest man had a nasty leer on his face.

"Boss said there might be someone wantin' to leave this place 'fore he an' Ridgeway got back. Looks as how he was right. What you doin' out this time of the mornin', gal?"

"That's frankly none of your business. Who is this 'boss' you mentioned?"

"I'll ask the questions, sister."

"I'm neither your gal nor your sister, you son of a bitch

184

Keep a civil tongue. I'll ask you again, what business do you have on Grover Ridgeway's land and who is your boss?"

"We're Range Detectives, which answers both questions. Now, we've got a few of our own. You scoutin' Ridgeway's place for your sodbuster daddy? Lookin' for a few free beeves to cull out?"

"I'm a guest of Grover Ridgeway. If you doubt it, check it out at the main house."

"Bullfeathers. Say, ain't that a Sioux dress yer a wearin'?"

"It is."

"Goddamned squaw sneakin' in here. We thought we'd learned you thievin' redskins a lesson."

"Hey, Len," a lanky, unshaven lout to the left of him called out. "She speaks English too good to be an Oglala. Fuckin' half-breed," he spat. "Maybe we oughtta send this one back to them lice-ridden bucks with a nice little white baby inside her, eh?"

"Yeah. Toby's got an idee, Len," a third hardcase piped up.

"We've got plenty of time," Toby added. "The big shots ain't due back before this afternoon."

A new light showed in Len's eyes. No longer cold and hostile, his hot, lustful gaze swept over Rebecca, mentally undressing her. Despite herself, she shuddered. He pricked his mount's flanks with spurs and moved closer.

Insolently he reached out and ran the back of his right hand down her cheek . . . and found that Rebecca had a surprise for him.

Her right hand flashed to her waist and came up with a small skinning knife. With a backhand stroke she sliced through skin, flesh and tendons on the back of Len's hand. He recoiled with a howl of pain and looked at the flood of red that washed from the wound.

"Oh, Jesus, boys!" he wailed in real panic. "She's done maimed me. I can't move my fingers. She's cut the tendons."

"Get her," Len snarled. "We'll have our fun with the bitch before we make her pay for that. Slim, you take care of

185

Len's hand."

The hard-faced regulators had started to move when they discovered Rebecca had more than one surprise for them. From her waist pouch she drew the .38 Baby Russian. In one smooth move the hammer came back and she squeezed off a round.

Hot lead made a meaty smack when it struck Toby between his bushy eyebrows. The bullet punched through to his brain and shut off enough consciousness so that he barely felt it when he fell to the ground.

"Die, you bitch!" Slim yelled.

It was the wrong thing to do, he discovered when his shout made him her next target. Rebecca's second shot smashed into his right biceps and his six-gun went flying. Her third made a neat black spot slightly to the right of his Bull Durham sack and stopped his heart when it reached the inside.

Glenn Leathers had had enough. He fled, cursing, with the helpless Len only half a length behind him. Rebecca sent another shot their way as a convincer. Quickly she reloaded from the loose rounds in her pouch and replaced her weapon. A slight trembling affected her hands.

The encounter had come too soon and developed too fast for her to think. Now she did, and she wished that two dead men didn't lie at her feet. Better them than me, the logical side of her mind suggested. Accepting that, she shrugged off the ominous feeling and gave rein to her skittery mount.

Chapter 21

Long, thin streamers, tinged dark gray on their bellies, lanced across the sky from northwest to northeast. They heralded the imminent arrival of snow. Before the day ended, Rebecca Caldwell surmised, there would be a blanket of white on the ground. The penetrating cold at the start of her journey had not lessened, and a sudden wind shift to the northeast added assurance to her conjecture. Another unpleasant surprise awaited her when she followed the road into one of the many gullies that cut the prairie.

Before she dropped below the level of the surrounding ground, seven men surged upward as though sprouting from the earth. At their head rode Alystaire Carmoody and Grover Ridgeway. Surprised, everyone reined in. Ridgeway trotted toward Rebecca, a troubled frown on his face.

"Sam, what is this? What's going on?" Grover asked with growing concern.

Desperate to get away with her precious information for both the Sioux and the governor, Rebecca chose to be blunt. In her anxiety, she dropped the honeysuckle-and-magnolia flavor from her voice and spoke naturally.

"Grover, I'm sorry, so sorry about this. My name isn't Samantha Waterhouse. It's Rebecca Caldwell. I can't explain it all now, but I have to leave. It's terribly important to a lot of people."

"But, Sam . . ."

From back among the riders came a whiney exclamation. "Hey, that's t'damned white squaw who shot Toby an' Slim an' cut ol' Len."

Baffled by this sudden change, Alystaire Carmoody nevertheless accepted the word of Glenn Leathers. "Take her boys," he commanded gruffly.

Although no gunman, Grover Ridgeway managed to clear leather with surprising speed. The ratcheting hammer of his .45 Colt made a loud sound in the cold early morning. Rebecca, too, drew her .38 Smith and Wesson. When he spoke, Ridgeway edged his words with steel.

"No one's taking anyone until we find out what this is about."

"Tell him, Glenn," Carmoody ordered, casting a fiery stare at Ridgeway.

"When I come up to y'all, I told you we got jumped. What I didn't say was that it had been a woman. This is the one."

"What were you doing on my property?" Grover asked gratingly.

"Mr. Carmoody put us there to see that no one decided to, ah, wander off while you was gone," Leathers answered sneeringly.

"Would you be kind enough to explain that, Alystaire."

"My reasoning seems obvious enough now. I never quite believed this, ah, southern belle of yours, Grover. She seemed too good to be true. Events have proven me out."

"Your man back there has a mighty big mouth for a would-be rapist," Rebecca challenged.

"What's this?" Grover Ridgeway demanded, bristling.

"That one and his friends stopped me near the main road," Rebecca explained. "They decided they had time enough to have their way with me before you got back. I, uh, convinced them otherwise."

"She killed two men," Leathers blurted out defensively.

188

"You didn't deny her other charge," Grover began angrily. "Out here we have a way of dealing with rustlers and rapists. You ought to be familiar enough with it, Leathers. You've hung a few."

On the defensive now, Leathers's weak voice raised half an octave. "You'd take the word of a squaw woman? A half-breed?"

"I'd take the word of the woman I love," Grover snapped back, unaware of the import of his declaration. "Someone get a rope ready."

"I'll not let you do this, Grover," Carmoody challenged. "He's one of my men and I won't believe he did such a thing."

"We're either going to hang this son of a bitch, or Samantha goes free. Which is it going to be?"

"Be reasonable, Grover," Carmoody urged.

"I *am* being reasonable, Alystaire. She's riding away from here right now, and I'm going with her to see no one follows, or we string up that cretin Leathers."

"You're outnumbered, Grover. Think this through. There are men out rounding up the rest of the regulators to attack the Sioux. Once they're all together, you two wouldn't stand a chance no matter where you went."

Rebecca raised the aim of her Baby Russian a bit. "Mr. Carmoody, if you want to live long enough to see all those *regulators,* I'd suggest you shut your mouth before I put a bullet in it."

Carmoody paled. He wiped a trembling hand across his face and directed pure hatred at Rebecca from his tiny pig eyes. He had no doubt that if a single one of his men moved, he'd be dead before he heard the shot. In desperation he fought to control the sound of his voice.

"Take it easy boys," he instructed. Then to the pair facing him, "I reckon you've won this round. You can ride on out. Remember this, though; we'll be after you. You've turned your coat, Ridgeway. You're a traitor. Before the sun sets, you'll pay for this."

"I'll not hold my breath," Grover answered back.

"You boys undo your gunleather and let them down easy," Rebecca demanded coldly. "Then your rifles. After that I want you to walk your mounts to the top of the gulley. Do it, or I'll kill your boss right where he sits."

Reluctantly, while Grover Ridgeway looked on in sheer awe, the Association gunhawks shed their weapons and kneed their horses forward. All the while, Rebecca Caldwell watched them carefully, the muzzle of her Smith and Wesson never wavering from Alystaire Carmoody's face. When the last had complied, she spoke again.

"Now you, Mr. Carmoody."

"You *bitch!*" Carmoody exploded.

"Now, now, Mr. Carmoody. Please don't use that sort of language. I wouldn't want people to think I killed you because you insulted me."

Face flushed, hands shaking from suppressed rage, Alystaire Carmoody obeyed. He gave a swinish grunt when he started off to join his men at the top of the rise. Two six-guns followed his progress until he rode out of sight. Rebecca dismounted and began unloading weapons.

"Give me a hand, will you, Grover?"

"Uh—sure."

They stored the ammunition in the saddle bags, the weapons Rebecca threw in the shallow, muddy creek. Then they mounted up. "I, ah, there's a lot I don't know," Grover Ridgeway started.

"Later. For now, let's put some distance between us and them," Rebecca countered.

Her story completed, Rebecca waited tensely. She expected no praise, feared condemnation. Across the low cookfire from her, Grover Ridgeway looked to be sunk in deep contemplation. Snow, mixed with seedlike sleet, hissed on the branches that formed the roofs of their two-part lean-to. The twin peaks nearly met over the small fire and provided relative warmth and comfort from the storm. At last he stirred, reaching around the flickering flames to take her hand.

"Now, damnit, don't expect flowery phrases or poetic prose. Not at a time like this. What I've got to say has to be done all at once, in a rush." Grover drew a deep breath, as though to fortify himself. "You've had your say and I've listened. Now I want to tell you this.

"I don't give a damn if you'd said you helped assassinate Lincoln. I love you, Sam, Rebecca, whatever your name is. You are a beautiful woman, a delightful person, and all too much fun to be around. I want to protect you with all my power for so long as we might live. If you say the Sioux are victims in this, I believe you. I—I suppose I've known that for some while now, anyway. There's . . . something rotten between Alystaire Carmoody and Colonel Peyton. A person can sense it when they're in the same room. If we ever really needed regulators for the Cattlemen's Association, there was no need for more than six. Not the thirty Carmoody has on hand now. And I don't like seeing the little guy get shoved around. These attacks on the small ranchers and farmers was an idea of Carmoody's and Delano's from the beginning, and I've always been opposed. So . . ."

Again Grover gulped in the air and squeezed Rebecca's hand even tighter. "So what I'm trying to say is this. I believe you, I love you, and I want you to be my wife."

Stunned, Rebecca sensed the color rushing to her face and the tears forming to sting her eyes. "Oh, Grover, I—I . . ." A bolt of unexplained laughter saved her from utter disaster. "I've never heard of such a proposal. It's wonderful. And I'm sure you mean it, but . . ."

"Don't!" Grover exploded, then hastened to her side of the fire. He took her in his arms and brought her head to his shoulder. "Don't refuse me. No matter what good reason you think you have, it's not good enough. I love you and I want to be with you always. Tomorrow, the next day, whenever things

191

have returned to normal, I'll feel the same. I'll ask you to marry me again, if you want. The truth is, now that I've come to know you, I can't let you go."

"Grover, Grover, between you and your sons, I don't know what to say or do. They're dear, sweet little boys, and you . . . ah, dear, wonderful Grover, you are the man every girl grows up dreaming about. You're not cut out to be a criminal, and I've known that all along. I'm so glad to hear how you feel about me. Only . . ."

Rebecca paused, aware her murmured words against his chest could not fail to arouse him. "You know about me now, my past, my determination to bring to justice those who have wronged me. How can you see me in the role of loving wife, tender mother, and mild-mannered housekeeper? How can you, after the way I handled those men this morning?"

"I drew on them first, remember?"

"Yes, my sweet thing, but I had every intention of killing Alystaire Carmoody if even one of his gunmen had blinked an eye. I've seen too many dead men, too much bloodshed ever to be completely domesticated. We can't begin. . . ."

"Then you'll be my *wild*, sweet wife," Grover interrupted.

"Oh, I want to. I so truly want to. A-ask me again, later, after this terrible situation is over and done."

"I will. Don't think you can get out of it so easily."

Rebecca looked up, eyes shining. "If you don't ask, you'll break my heart."

Rebecca and Grover made one stop before turning due north toward the Šayaota encampment. Doctor Milburn Sager objected at first about being taken from his regular practice for a long-range mission of mercy. Grover Ridgeway reminded the doctor of an old obligation and he consented readily. When the trio topped the last rise to the bowllike valley where the Oglala camped, Rebecca noticed the shrunken size of the village and her heart felt leaden.

"Something's happened," she remarked quietly.

"How do you know?"

"The lodges. There must have been twenty, twenty-five more when I left. This is not good. We'll have to hurry. I want to find out."

The *eyenapah* called out their arrival, and Lone Wolf, Hump, and Whirlwind met her in front of the new chief's lodge. Containing her anxiety, Rebecca quickly explained about the doctor and asked that he be taken to Sweetgrass's tipi to examine Tipsila Ce. Then she asked the dreaded question.

"What happened? Where is Two Bulls, and the rest of the young men?"

"The council split evenly. Two Bulls and those who wanted war struck camp and went their own way," Lone Wolf explained. "It's getting harder everyday for Hump to hold the people together."

"We have to do something about this at once," Rebecca responded. "This is Grover Ridgeway. He's come along to explain what's behind all the trouble. We'll go to the governor. But first, Hump," she addressed the chief, "you must call the council. A man named Carmoody is preparing to attack your village with some thirty men."

When the council gathered, Rebecca swiftly outlined all she knew. Her statements were verified by Grover Ridgeway. Ridgeway then informed them of the Army plans to march at once on the Šayaota encampment. Angry mutters rose. The men debated for a long while, then summoned Rebecca and Grover before them.

"This is a bad thing," Hump began. "Many people could die. Some of our people feel that they can't trust you. That you have turned to your white side. I don't think this is a true thing. Can you and this man go to the soldiers and explain? Can you speak to the Little White Father for us?"

"Yes. And gladly, Hump. But we must hurry."

"Take what you need. Ponies, food, warriors to protect you on the journey, all are yours. Make fast to do it."

"We will," Rebecca promised.

Before the noon meal, a small caravan, consisting of Rebecca, Grover, Lone Wolf, Broken Hand, and five warriors rode from camp. Their journey to Pierre would take two precious days.

Legs spraddled, Alystaire Carmoody stood on the porch of Branch Delano's ranch house. Fists on hips, he recited from memory a list of names, designating these men to ride eastward and join up with the Army column advancing on the Sioux. The remainder, he informed them, would come with him to attack the Oglala village from another direction.

"What about the ones who've been doin' the raidin'? They're to the west of us," Jubal Coulter, the new leader of the regulators said.

"We'll not worry about them. We'll finish off their home base and let the Army take care of the warriors. You boys keep one thing in mind. Once we get the damned Sioux out of here, each of you is going to have four square miles of prime land to call your own. Title guaranteed by the Dakota Cattlemen's Association."

A wild cheer answered him.

"Let Baccus's sons be not dismayed, but join me every jovial blade, to sing and dance and lend us aid and help me with the chorus!"

Oh, God, Lt. Joe Demarris thought with a sinking feeling. Lieutenant Colonel Peyton had completely lost control. The entire regiment walked their mounts across the parade ground, toward the gates, in a column of fours, while the band played and the men sang the "Garry Owen", the regimental song of Custer's Seventh Cavalry. A three-day ride ahead of them to the Red Top Lodge encampment—and what to expect when they got there? Let it not be Peyton's own Little Big Horn, the

194

young officer silently prayed.

His preoccupation did not prevent Lieutenant Demarris from noticing that Captain Stanley, the provost marshal, who held the salute for the departing troops, had what appeared to be a mocking smirk on his face. Why would that be? Demarris wondered.

"Two Bulls! Two Bulls!" A young Oglala warrior's pony sprayed dust and rocks as he bolted into the ring of lodges, calling for the war chief. The lathered mount heaved and shuddered when brought to a halt.

"What is it?"

"The white men who want our lands ride in strength toward the old campsight."

"You're sure?" Two Bulls scowled, arms folded across his chest.

"They all went to the place Big Nose burned. The one that's their leader spoke to them. Then part rode to where the sun comes up, while the others went with him. They'll be at the camp on the Earth Smoke in two days."

"Now we can attack their lodges, burn them, kill the stinking meat animals," one warrior suggested.

"Many of our women and children will die," suggested another. "That's not our way."

Two Bulls took only a moment to decide. "To your ponies. Gather your weapons. We'll ride to strike these false men in the rear. They'll die to the last man!"

Yips and howls answered him as the vengeance-hungry braves hurried to comply.

Chapter 22

Meadowlarks warbled in the frosty morning, braving the snow to feed on grass seeds and the few remaining hearty insects. Crows and hawks made lazy spirals, seeking nourishment that might expose itself on the white mantle that covered the ground. Slate-gray, the sky hung low, and occasional flurries of flakes tumbled downward. Back three miles, well beyond the ridge, the regulators grumbled in a cold camp while Alystaire Carmoody and a knowledgeable frontiersman named Smiley scouted the Oglala encampment below in the dish valley. They had made a count of lodges, and Smiley frowned with dislike.

"We agree to it bein' twenty-seven lodges," Smiley murmured. "You figger two warriors to a lodge, that's usual. Fifty-four to our sixteen ain't exactly desirable odds."

"There were more lodges when we attacked before."

"Yep. An' you hit 'em at night, shot up the place a little and ran like hell after. This is gonna be a pitched battle. We'd best have some stayin' power."

"Maybe I shouldn't have split up the force we had," Carmoody reflected rhetorically.

"You're the one in charge. Been up to me, I'd notta done it."

"We have to draw back then, and wait for the Army to get here."

"Makes sense. What about them bucks that's out on the prowl?"

197

In good humor for the first time since Grover Ridgeway's defection, Carmoody slapped the former Army scout on the shoulder. "Smiley, as you're fond of sayin', there are just some things we can't know about until they bites us in the ass. If they split off for some reason, their chances of coming back here are slim at best. Fact is, we should be worried about our spreads. They get wind of our being gone and anything could happen."

"The boys ain't gonna like that."

"Not those who are in the Association. These rip-snorters you and Aaron hired on haven't a care in the world."

"Then we wait."

"That's what we do."

If everything went well, Lieutenant Colonel Bryce Peyton thought to himself as the regiment trotted along over the gentle swell of the prairie, he'd soon be free of the curse of Captain Duncan Stanley. The bonus promised by Alystaire Carmoody for the successful extermination of the free Sioux would do quite nicely. In part, at least.

Hell, he didn't want land in Dakota Territory. In fact, he never wanted to see the godforsaken place again. Not even if he owned a dozen square miles of it. A couple of one-section parcels to live on and develop should satisfy any man's needs for retirement. He'd offer the two sections to Stanley, in exchange for all of the incriminating evidence, then sell off the rest to land-hungry settlers.

Then, later, after they'd both retired, he'd come back and kill Stanley to seal his lips forever. No, he figured, no one could pass up a prize like that. Only another day's ride and then he'd have the Sioux at his mercy. The ill-disciplined border trash Carmoody had sent to him rankled, though. They were a bad influence on the troops. He'd use them all right. In the forefront of the charge, like so much cannon fodder. Wouldn't hurt to knock down some of Carmoody's power.

His demands had become too great. Everything hinged on a good outcome for this venture. If he contained the surviving Sioux and put them on the reservations, he'd be a hero to headquarters. If he failed, he'd better hope he didn't live to face the court-martial.

Lt. Joe Demarris watched his commanding officer with no lessening of his anxiety. Lieutenant Colonel Peyton seemed outwardly in control. Yet his occasional outbursts at soldiers for the mildest of offenses, that frequent nervous tic that set the corner of his mouth to twitching, his muttered, subvocal conversations with men long dead, which he held in the supposed privacy of his tent, all pointed toward an unstable mind hovering on the verge of insanity.

How much of this had to do with the death of his friend, Arnulf Larsen? Joe Demarris wished he could answer that. Never on his worst day would Arnie have considered suicide. Not when he knew he was right. Joe wondered, too, what answer he would give to First Sergeant Thompkins. He had considered the noncom's request and was trying to formulate some sort of plan that would expose all of the irregularities, although he had not yet come up with a satisfactory manner of dealing with it all.

That, too, he decided, would have to wait.

A covey of quail was flushed from its warm nest below the snow at the approach of the column of war ponies. Wings whirring, they sped away in a fan-shaped spray. Two Bulls nodded at them.

"The good-to-eat grass-birds know we are hunting," he shouted laughingly to Eagle Claw.

"It's not they whom we hunt," Eagle Claw responded, grinning.

"Our scouts will return when the Sky Father is high overhead," Two Bulls remarked unnecessarily. "Then we'll know where the evil whites wait for us so they can die."

"Are we going to kill a lot of them, Father?" Tommy Archer asked excitedly as he rode up to join the two men.

"*You* are going to hold horses, tend camp, and do all the other things apprentice warriors do, Mahtociqala," his adopted parent admonished. "The days of your fighting our enemies are yet to come."

"Awh . . ." Tommy pouted.

Two Bulls softened a bit, gave the boy a friendly cuff. "I've only just found you, my son. I have no desire to lose you to a wasicun bullet. Now go back and ride with the other boys."

"Yes, Father."

"He'll make a great warrior," Eagle Claw observed after Tommy's departure.

"That he might. Yet, he is a white boy."

"Not when he shot the one who tried to stab my daughter."

Two Bulls caught a certain note in his friend's voice. He cocked an eyebrow and produced a crooked grin. "You'd look kindly on his efforts if he were to bring horses to your lodge some season yet to come?"

Eagle Claw grunted. "I would. Don't you go telling him that; he thinks himself older in too many ways as it is."

"No. He'll not hear it from me. Such speculations of joining our families is for a long talk around a winter's fire. First we have these cursed whites to deal with. And Small Bear is right, we'll kill them all."

Midmorning of the second day found Rebecca and her small party twenty-five miles west of Pierre. A well-traveled road had replaced the faint trails they had followed until now. Lone Wolf and Burns His Lodge, who had gone ahead a ways to locate water, returned to inform the others that another band of travelers of about their size was headed toward them.

"Who could it be?" Rebecca inquired.

"We'd better hope it's not more of Carmoody's regulators," Grover Ridgeway offered.

"We'll find out in another ten minutes," Lone Wolf replied.

"There's no place we can get out of sight," Rebecca observed. "It might be best to wait here and let them come to us."

No suitable alternative appeared, so the determined little band spread out for maximum field of fire and waited the coming of the strangers. Grover Ridgeway took the opportunity to talk with Rebecca

"I'm still sick at heart over that little boy. You say Colonel Peyton is supposed to have ordered his troops to fire?"

"Colonel Peyton *did* order his soldiers to fire. I was there. They were shooting at me as well. They killed Ptasan Okiye and bayoneted Tipsi—he's the wounded child you saw. A white boy, Tommy Archer, rescued him."

"Really? What happened to him?"

"He's with his adopted family. With the hostiles under Two Bulls."

"My God!"

"It's not so bad as all that, Grover. Tommy has a strong sense of right and wrong. He'd not fight his own kind, at least not innocent people. As to the Army, or Carmoody's regulators, I wouldn't take any bets."

"How old is this lad?"

"Eleven. And, Grover, he's already killed one of the Range Detectives. It was a right courageous fellow who was trying to knife a little girl." Rebecca went on to describe the circumstances regarding Tommy Archer and concluded with the latest information she'd obtained.

"Mrs. Archer is reported prostrate with grief. More likely relief. Her past record of harsh punishment and abuse to the child are a matter of record. Her husband has so far made no commitment one way or the other. Remarkable that a man could have so mousy a character."

"Then you would approve of this boy's staying with the Oglala?"

Rebecca gave him a gentle smile. "I lived with these same

Oglala for five years, remember?"

"You did mention that," Grover agreed. "With all that's happened, I'm afraid it slipped my mind."

A spurt of relief washed over Rebecca Caldwell. If those years, so fraught with meaning for her, held no more importance to him than that, his judgement of her might not be so harsh, after all.

"Riders coming," Lone Wolf called.

Small, dark forms against the gray sky grew larger and more distinct. Within a minute, Rebecca could recognize the squat form of Philo Bates. The short, bowlegged marshal raised in his stirrups and waved to them. In a matter of seconds the two groups joined.

"We were just on our way to find you," Bates declared. "This here's the territorial attorney general. He's got warrants for the arrest of every member of the Cattlemen's Association, along with some in blank for those regulators they hired. The governor's also got on to the Army, back at department headquarters, to launch an investigation into Colonel Peyton's actions regarding your peace mission. Ah . . ." Bates paused a moment, puzzled by Rebecca's expression. "You don't seem too happy about all this?"

"Well, we can't say it's too little. But I'm afraid it came too late."

"How's that, Miss Rebecca?"

"Philo, the Army's in the field and so are the regulators. This is Mr. Grover Ridgeway. He's come along with us to verify that the two forces are planning an attack on the Sayaota main village."

Bates worked on that information a moment, his eyes bright with a keen glint. "There's enough warriors in that village to stand off such a force until we can get there, ain't there?"

"Not anymore," Rebecca said. "The council split over the issue of another try for peace or war. Many of the warriors went with Two Bulls. There's only half the strength, or less, to defend the village."

202

"Damn. We'd best not be wastin' time, then. You folks ready to ride back with us?"

"You can be sure of that."

Rebecca had exchanged the horse she had taken from the Ridgeway ranch for her Appaloosie stallion, Ŝila, and she knew the animal had the endurance for the ordeal they would face. The others would have to do the best they could. As a result, her answer sounded more ominous than she'd intended.

"We'll have to make the best time we can, or there's bound to be a disaster."

Chapter 23

The prospect of losing his benefactor troubled Capt. Duncan Stanley. After the regiment had departed he brooded over finding some means to protect his newfound source of revenue. An opportunity presented itself in the form of half a dozen regulators who straggled into the fort too late to join the main column. He would lead them to where they were expected, Stanley informed them, and made preparations to absent himself from the post.

On the trail, his carefully thought-out comments persuaded the gunmen that their best hope lay in joining with their boss instead of with the Army. Accordingly, they diverted their course cross-country to skirt the Oglala encampment to the south and locate Carmoody. Once they had, and Carmoody had expressed his gratitude for the reinforcements, Captain Stanley wasted no time in approaching his intended new victim.

"There's, ah, something I wish to discuss with you in private, Mr. Carmoody," Stanley began obliquely.

"What's that?"

"Can we go off a ways first?"

"I suppose so."

Together, the rancher and the cavalry officer strolled over the low prairie. Some fifty yards from the regulator camp,

Stanley came to a halt. Eyeing his prospect carefully, he made a complete explanation of what he knew, how he'd come to know it, and the implications for the future. Carmoody's face hardened a little more at each sentence of the revelation, causing some consternation for Stanley. He exhibited considerable nervousness by the time he came to his pitch.

"So, as I'm sure you can see, it would be disastrous for both you and Colonel Peyton were this to be revealed. So far, the protections I have prepared regarding my knowledge of Bryce Peyton's illegal activities have no mention of you by name. Now, I'm a reasonable man. Any, ah, continuing relationship between you and me could prove difficult for both of us. Therefore, I'm prepared to grant you complete immunity from any possible future investigation for a moderate consideration. Say, a single payment of five thousand dollars?"

"I, too, am a reasonable man," Carmoody answered in a menacing purr. "The idea of paying a leech like you extortion money for the rest of my life, or even for one time, is repugnant to me. Which leaves me but one option."

With terrible clarity, Captain Stanley saw the one flaw in his plan of obtaining another source of wealth. He had been entirely too candid. He should never have revealed that he hadn't identified Carmoody by name. Desperately, as Alystaire Carmoody drew his six-gun, Duncan Stanley tried to cover his error.

"You don't understand," he cried in a braying voice. "If something happens to me, the evidence goes to department headquarters. Your partner in this affair will have his crimes known to everyone."

"Frankly, I don't care what happens to Bryce. Once he's served his purpose by disposing of the Sioux, our association is ended."

"When Bryce has his activities exposed, he'll naturally incriminate you."

"No, he'll not, Captain. There's an old saying: 'Dead men tell no tales.'"

Why, why had he let his greed bring him to such a pass? Duncan Stanley, captain U.S. Cavalry, had only a fleeting moment to consider this as he watched the hammer fall on Alystaire Carmoody's Colt and saw the bloom of flame at the muzzle that lanced toward him behind the big .45 slug that ended his life.

"Bury this trash somewhere," Carmoody commanded the men who came running at the sound of the shot. "So far as we know, he never got here, right?"

"Our scouts have located Mr. Carmoody's camp, sir," Lt. Joseph Demarris reported to Lieutenant Colonel Peyton. "It's situated to the south, at a right angle to our own approach, some five miles from the hostiles' village."

"Excellent. Had they anything else to report, Lieutenant?"

"Yes, sir. Mr. Carmoody's compliments, and he'll be ready to attack when you give the word, sir."

"And now, White Buffalo, we bloody the rest of your people," Peyton muttered to himself. He caught the dereliction and coughed to cover himself. "Very well, then. Send him word that we will attack tomorrow at dawn."

"Yes, sir." Demarris saluted and rode away.

"You'll have your revenge now, George. Oh, how I'll make them pay," Peyton said softly, with trembling fervor.

Hump received the delegation from the governor with gratitude. Here was the way to peace. What he had hoped for, prayed to the Great Spirit to bring about, had come to pass. The news that two hostile forces lay within less than ten miles of the camp he accepted with less pleasure.

"You have all done well," he told the whites gathered before his lodge. "Now the council must meet. We'll fight to defend ourselves," he explained to the attorney general. "But we do not attack."

"I understand, and so does the governor, that you have been provoked beyond what any reasonable person should be expected to endure without retaliation," the politico began.

Rebecca's translation pleased Hump. He smiled and extended his hand to Norman Hastings. The attorney general clasped it tightly, then continued his prepared statement.

"The matter of the train cannot be forgotten. Two people lost their lives; many were wounded or injured in the wreck. However, the lives lost and damage done to your people by these, ah, regulators for the Cattlemen's Association are a mitigating circumstance. That will all have to be worked out with the proper authorities. For my own part, I carry along orders from the Army and the governor to cease all hostilities. The soldiers will not attack you, nor will the civilians."

"You should be telling them this," Hump replied rather bluntly.

"I admit that I am remiss in that. It will be remedied tomorrow morning. First, though, I wanted to assure you of a peaceful solution."

"My heart is light at your words."

"Thank you, Chief Hump."

"Now the council meets. We know you talk straight, but we can't trust the others. Our safety is at stake."

"So's ours," Hastings replied. "Because we'll be staying here."

In slow, gentle transition, dawn spread across the prairie, in marked contrast to the deadly works of man that went forward on this new day. Bit chains jingled and the cavalry mounts snorted and stamped, as though aware of what would soon come. Under strict noise discipline, the men muttered their usual complaints and went about making ready. Lt. Col. Bryce Peyton wanted to sing. He hadn't felt so excited in years. When all was in readiness, he swung atop his black charger and settled himself in the saddle.

"You men in the band, keep your instruments with you. Be ready to fall in on our left flank when I give the command to charge. Forward in a column of fours, ho!" Peyton commanded.

The troops fell in line in perfect parade ground order. Each man had tended to his weapons, insured an ample supply of ammunition, and grumbled as he polished all his bright work. Now they made a splendid display cantering lightly across the plain, toward the distant rim that separated them from the hostile Sioux. Few among them thought fearful thoughts of death, or maiming, or worse, capture. Confidence remained high.

Two miles left to go. Then one. Then the slow walk up the rising slope. The whispered commands flew along the column with their own thrill of eagerness.

"Form two ranks to the front . . . Ho! Dress right. Prepare to draw carbines . . . Draw!"

Fifty yards to go. At last the top. Spread below they saw the concentric circles of the sleeping village.

"Bandsmen to the left flank."

Peyton again: "Trumpeter, sound the *Charge*."

Sharp-edged notes rippled on the cold morning air.

"At the gallop . . . *CHARGE!*"

"Up and get movin'. You there, outta that blanket. Get up!" The command went around the small camp of hired guns.

Alystaire Carmoody stood by a low fire sipping coffee. He already wore a battered white linen duster and a floppy hat. Eagerness made him jittery. He sloshed the coffee when another of the Association members spoke from behind.

"Good day for a slaughter, eh, Alystaire?"

"It'll do nicely. C'mon and get some coffee."

Within an hour breakfast had been eaten and every man made ready. At a quick trot, they moved out for the rim of the valley. All were hardened fighting men and had eaten heavy breakfasts in anticipation of a difficult day. Many contemplated the cash bonus they had coming, or the land they could receive. Others thought of women; those they would buy later on and those they would rape in the village below. The rise became more apparent after an hour's walk, and the horses began to labor.

A few yards below the crest, Carmoody called a halt. "Spread out into a single line. Use your carbines first, then six-guns." The whispered instructions went back along the line.

Silently the men complied. When the last fell into line, Carmoody motioned them forward. The regulators topped the ridge and walked their mounts downslope some thirty yards. Before them they saw the many lodges of the Oglala. Off to their right, half a mile away, they dimly made out the dark ribbons of blue that identified the cavalry. Suddenly the brilliant notes of a bugle destroyed dawn's quiet. Cymbals crashed and a band struck up the "Garry Owen".

"CHARGE!"

"That's it, boys. Goooo geet 'em!" Carmoody bellowed.

Two Bulls's eyes widened at the sight of so many soldiers. At least his men, approaching from behind by half a mile, would put up a good fight. Then he saw the thicker clusters of men around the guns-that-shoot-far. A cold lump formed in his stomach. The soldiers would use them against the lodges in the village. Many women and children would die. His dread changed to anger. Quickly he revised his plans.

He and his men would swing wide behind the concealment of the ridge. Come in at an angle. Kill the soldiers at the far-shooting guns. Carefully he crawled backward and hurried to meet his men. The soldiers would not be to the top of the ridge for some while. There would still be time.

When Two Bulls rejoined his band of twenty-eight warriors, he made quick explanations, and the Oglala swung northward to come in behind the soldiers. The ponies trotted faster with each passing minute. A thin slice of orange showed on the horizon, and Two Bulls urged greater speed.

"We will not be in time," Whirlwind stated flatly.

"We will do what we must," Two Bulls replied. "There, near the top of the ridge. We'll cross over there and sweep through the soldiers."

All too much time seemed to pass while the warriors advanced to their objective. Two Bulls urged them to a gallop, and the hard-working horses protested with snorts and grunts. All the same the slope was bested at last, and Two Bulls waved for his followers to spread out for the attack.

Sharp notes sounded from the bugle an instant before Two Bulls raised in his stirrups and shouted a defiant challenge at his enemy. *"Hu ihpeya wicayapo!"*

"Huka hey!" echoed from twenty-eight throats.

Watching from the encampment, Rebecca Caldwell saw the soldiers deploy, then the arrival of the regulators. Quietly the word went through the village to make ready. What fighting men remained mounted up and took their weapons to hand. Then a large number of Sioux warriors appeared on the rim of the valley. It had to be Two Bulls, Rebecca thought with growing excitement. The bugle's clarion call cut through the morning dark. Faintly she heard a voice command the charge. Waves of men swept down along the inner slope toward the valley floor.

"It's time to go," she announced to Lone Wolf and U.S. Marshal Bates.

All around them tense people watched the approach of sure death and destruction. Only Philo Bates retained a grin of anticipation. Under one arm he held a large contraption he felt certain would gain them the attention they needed.

"Ready whenever you are," he curtly informed Rebecca.

Only seconds remained before the three contingents would clash. Rebecca nodded tightly and the small party rode out.

Lone Wolf carried a huge white banner, attached to a lance decorated with fully a hundred white heron feathers. With Rebecca slightly ahead, the trio cleared the edge of the village and cantered toward the place where the conflict had to meet at any moment. Five warriors followed them.

They reached the spot first, and Philo Bates struck a lucifer, waited for it to stop flaring, and touched the flame to the end of a piece of fuse. He then hurled the object he'd been carrying far out toward the advancing soldiers.

With a loud roar, it exploded. "That ought to get their attention," he remarked smugly. Then he trotted a bit closer to the approaching troops, who had slowed their charge at the blast of smoke and bright flash. Commandingly he raised one hand.

"Hold back there!" he yelled, loud and clear. Turning, he did the same for the regulators. "This is U.S. Marshal Philo Bates. I've orders here from the Department of Dakota and from the governor of the territory to cease what you're doing."

Uneasily, the three sides came to unsteady halts and eyed each other across less than fifty yards' distance.

Chapter 24

"What t'hell!" Alystaire Carmoody's explosive utterance rang loudly in the rapt silence that followed the marshal's announcement. "Shoot that son of a bitch and let's get on with it," he shouted toward Bryce Peyton.

"The Little Father from the *wasicun* village on Grass-Lodge Creek has sent marks on paper to help you," Rebecca called out in Lakota to the warriors who had halted in confusion behind Two Bulls. "The *itancan* of the white *akicita* is here to punish the men who attacked your villages."

At Rebecca's nod, Philo Bates removed a warrant from his coat pocket and began to read in a loud voice. ". . . do hereby order the arrest for criminal conspiracy to defraud the territorial government of land and to do murder to the Indian occupants of the said land, and to deprive legitimate homesteaders of their land through murder, mayhem, and other means, the following persons: Alystaire Carmoody, Branch Delano, Harold Sonderson . . ." He continued until the list had been completed. Following that, he read the warrants for murder and rustling against the regulators, supplying names where possible.

"You'll not be arresting us," Carmoody shouted back. "We've done nothing wrong. Those are all based on lies, told to the governor by Injun lovers."

"Would you call Grover Ridgeway an Injun lover?" Bates responded.

"Hell, no. Why ain't his name on that paper?" Branch Delano came back.

A sudden stir began at the edge of the village and the defenders parted to allow Grover Ridgeway to ride clear. Beside him came Tipsila Ce, still weak and pale, but able to ride his pony. He'd been tightly bandaged by Doctor Sager, and Rebecca saw him wince as he and Ridgeway joined the small party at the focal point.

"Because I provided much of the information on which those warrants were based," Ridgeway answered. "It's gone too far, Alystaire. You, too, Colonel. This boy you had nearly murdered was the final turning point for me. Marshal Bates has new orders he was unstructed to bring to you, from department headquarters. They make a point of your doing absolutely nothing at this time or in the future to harm the Red Top Lodge Oglalas. You are to return to Camp Cullen and prepare yourself for a board of inquiry. So give it up now."

"I forgive the soldier who hurt me and I don't want any fighting, anymore," little Tipsila Ce called out in Lakota, in a clear, soprano voice, weakened by his long ordeal. "Let the soldiers go home."

"*CAAA-PAAA!*" Tommy Archer's squeaky voice shrilled from the top of the rim. "You're alive!"

Beaver, the boy so long called Turnip Penis, grinned and waved his arm.

"Colonel, do you understand the orders that I'm giving to you?" Philo Bates demanded.

"Uh, yes, sir. I do." Bitterness and defeat strangled Bryce Peyton's voice.

"Then I'll ride forward and hand them to you."

"C-come ahead."

By God, there's justice left in this world after all, Lt. Joe Demarris thought with relief.

After delivering the sealed orders to Lieutenant Colonel

Peyton, Philo Bates turned to the hot, angry face of Alystaire Carmoody. "Carmoody, this is the last chance for you and the others to surrender peacefully."

"We'll not surrender, and there's not enough of you to take us," Carmoody yelled in defiance.

"You're wrong there, Carmoody. I'll have the Army help make the arrests.

Astonishingly, in light of his orders, Lieutenant Colonel Peyton rounded on Marshal Bates and snarled at him. "I'll not do a single thing to aid you in this travesty."

Faced with a momentary impasse, Marshal Bates looked around him, brow wrinkled in outward show of the most unconventional of internal debates. At last he nodded his head, as though assuring someone else, and took a deep breath. Waving his arm to encompass the village and the warriors on the slope, he called loud and clear.

"Then yer all deputized!"

When Rebecca translated the meaning of this, a wild whoop went up from all the Šayaota. Those with Two Bulls kicked their ponies into motion and swept away from the soldiers, heading for the men not in blue uniforms. The warriors from the village joined in also, racing up the slope toward Alystaire Carmoody and his gang of cutthroats.

"*You turncoat bastard!*" Carmoody shrieked, on the edge of insane rage.

Carmoody's six-gun flashed in the weak morning sunlight. He thrust it forward and fired a shot that ripped into Grover Ridgeway's chest. Rebecca looked on in horror, her vision partly obscured, as Ridgeway fell from the saddle. A .44 Smith American roared in Rebecca's hand an instant after Carmoody discharged his weapon. Fate protected the enraged rancher when the milling regulators came between him and Rebecca's bullet.

The slug pulped an anonymous gunhawk's brain and splashed the contents of his head out the opposite side. He folded at the waist and lay along his horse's neck, pouring blood. Awakened from their shock at the sudden turn of events, the remaining hardcases began to exchange shots with the Indians who were intent on apprehending them. Carmoody made a try for Rebecca, only to have his mount jostled and the shot go wild. A moment later the Oglala warriors swarmed over the resisting gunmen.

Hell held court for the next five minutes. Men fought at arm's distance. Some shrieked and died horribly, arrows through their chests, throats, or stomachs, bullets smashing bone and tissue, skulls crushed by stone war clubs. Unexpectedly Lieutenant Colonel Bryce Peyton broke from the line of unmoving soldiers and raced his mount into the fray on the side of his friend Alystaire Carmoody.

Uttering a wild cry, Peyton pierced the side of Big Nose with his saber and the warrior fell away with a soundless cry. A short distance away a heavy Sharps boomed in the hands of Two Bulls, and the .56-caliber ball exploded Lt. Col. Bryce Peyton's head into a red mist. Rebecca worked her way to where she had a clear shot and unhorsed another regulator with a bullet that stopped his heart. With command of the troops disintegrating, Lt. Joe Demarris took charge.

"A Company, stand fast. The rest of the regiment reform on the crest of the ridge. Trumpeter, sound Recall."

Shards of bugle notes sprayed the air and set the troops in motion, away from the fighting. Some grumbled to themselves, others secretly felt relief. Lieutenant Demarris watched the withdrawal with his features set in rigid neutrality. When the maneuver had been completed, he summoned his first sergeant.

"Sergeant Thompkins, under Article Twenty-six of the Articles of War, entitled 'Aid to Civilian Authorities', we have an obligation to assist the U.S. marshal in the arrest of these miscreants. Get the men ready to move out."

"Yes, sir. Ah, but beggin' the lieutenant's pardon, sir, aren't you forgetting the Twelfth Article, about assuming command?"

"Oh, that's right. Consider it done, in light of the colonel's demise. Now be quick about it."

"Yes, sir."

Before the soldiers could get into motion, the regulators broke and began to run from the battle. Howling after them came the Sioux warriors. Off to one side, toward the distant line of watching troops, Rebecca saw Branch Delano and Alystaire Carmoody attempting to escape pursuit and find safety among the Army's ranks. She dug heels into Šila's flanks and pounded after them.

Branch Delano saw her coming first. He turned in his saddle and fired a wild shot that cracked over her head. Accurate shooting from the moving platform of a horse's back was the stuff of dreams. Rebecca had been told that by a number of experts, including Frank James. She had no trouble believing it as she watched her own shot go far from the mark. Delano continued on.

Rebecca grimly pursued him. Delano sent another round cracking past. Abruptly Rebecca reined in, took a steady two-hand hold on her Smith and Wesson American and squeezed the trigger. The powder smoke had not cleared when she saw Branch Delano throw his arms wide, arch his back, and flip backward off his surging horse. One down, she thought darkly. Now for Carmoody, the bastard who'd shot the man she loved.

Alystaire Carmoody had never known such utter defeat. All his life he had been gifted with success and excellence. Here in this forsaken valley of Dakota Territory his bright future had turned to bitter ash. In the moments after he had shot Grover Ridgeway he felt a soaring confidence. Then the Sioux swarmed over them and his men began dying. Not since he'd been a small child had he known such fear. The grunt driven from Branch Delano by the impact of a slug only spurred his terror. No matter where he looked, he had no place to go. Unwillingly, he turned his head to look behind him.

Carmoody's eyes widened in shock when he saw the speeding figure of Ridgeway's woman less than three lengths behind him. Her fierce blue eyes seemed to stab at him and he shuddered involuntarily at the ugly twist of her mouth. The lust for his blood had transformed her.

"You're mine, Carmoody," she yelled. "You'll not go to the gallows. You'll not even spend time in prison. I'm going to finish you right here."

"Don't!" he pleaded, despite his urgent desire to conserve strength and speed.

Desperate, he fired two close-spaced shots that missed by several feet. Half a length more had been pared from his lead. He saw the black muzzle of the eight-and-three-eighths-inch barreled Smith American raise toward him, big as a Parisian sewer pipe. He started to cry out for mercy when yellow-orange flame spurted from it.

His plea turned to anguish when the hot slug cut a deep gouge across the top of his right shoulder. Reflexively his fingers opened and he dropped his six-gun. Another full length had been closed, he saw with rising panic. Biting his lip against the pain, Carmoody bent to draw his saddle gun. The Winchester came free easily and he levered a round into the chamber. Desperately he reined his mount to the side in an attempt to line up on his pursuer.

Šila reacted instantly, jinking in the opposite direction and lining his rider up for a clear shot. The .44 Smith and Wesson crashed again.

Alystaire Carmoody howled in pain when the slug struck the receiver of his rifle and ripped it from his grasp. He had only one weapon left, a long, thin-bladed knife he habitually carried as a memento of his days in New Orleans. Fighting his confusion and fright, he reached for it.

Before Carmoody could recover, Šila made two bounding jumps forward and crashed his chest into that of the rancher's mount. Carmoody went sprawling, his knife, free of the scabbard, landing a good two feet from where he struck the ground. Rebecca check-reined Šila and swung from the saddle. Spraddle-legged, she stood over the corrupt rancher, the Smith American held casually hammer cocked, muzzle centered on his forehead.

"You wouldn't shoot an unarmed man," he blurted, more a plea than a statement.

"You're right, I wouldn't. But your knife's right there. So close, isn't it?" A grin spread on Rebecca's powder-grimed face as Alystaire Carmoody eyed his weapon and his mind began to digest the problem.

"I know what you're thinking. Did she fire five or six rounds? In the heat of battle, it's hard to keep count. I might have an empty gun here. Feel up to trying it?"

Sweat beaded Carmoody's expanse of forehead and bald pate. His eyes darted nervously between the menacing woman and his knife. If he got it in his hands and she did have an empty weapon, it would be over in seconds. He'd not lived through three years in the dangerous alleys and dockyards of New Orleans by being an amateur. Sure, it was a gamble, but it was the best thing he'd been offered since the day had begun, so short a time ago. Reflexively he made a hesitant, incomplete movement toward the blade.

"Go on, try it. What have you got to lose?"

Her cold, merciless taunting goaded him. With a yell of desperation, Alystaire Carmoody made a wild dive for his knife. Pain speared through his chest from his injured shoulder as he rolled over. Yet he came up with the keen-edged dagger in his hand, still alive!

Then the world turned bright white inside Alystaire Carmoody's head and he heard only faintly the horrendous roar of the detonating .44 Smith and Wesson.

Within twenty minutes of the time Alystaire Carmoody died, the last fleeing regulator had been chased down and brought back a captive. The fighting ended. Rebecca returned to the encampment and to her great joy and astonishment found Grover Ridgeway being treated by Doctor Milburn Sager, who had revived young Beaver.

"He got it in the shoulder," the gruff medico informed her. "Up close to the joint. Won't be doin' much with that arm for a while."

In her joy, Rebecca ignored the physician and dropped to her knees beside the pallet of buffalo robes and covered Grover's face with kisses and hot, grateful tears. "My dear, dear Grover. Oh, I was so afraid, so terribly afraid. And so angry at Alystaire Carmoody."

"Carmoody?" Grover asked weakly.

"I killed him."

"My God."

Grover's eyes closed, and Doctor Sager firmly steered Rebecca out of the lodge. It did little for Rebecca's peace of mind.

Lt. Joe Demarris rode down to the village and greeted Deputy U.S. Marshall Philo Bates. "My compliments, Marshal Bates, and it seems like your task has been accomplished."

A silent ring of Oglala formed around the lawman and the soldier.

"Yours, too, Lieutenant."

"Yes . . . that it has. We'll be forming up and marching back to Camp Cullen. Ah . . . I'd like the body of Colonel Peyton to return with us, if I may?"

"Certainly, we've no hold on him, dead or alive," Bates agreed.

"Thank you. First Sergeant!"

"Sir!" Thompkins responded crisply from a few yards away.

"Form a detail to tend to the colonel's body."

"Yes, sir."

"I'm sorry all this happened," Demarris said sincerely to Hump and Two Bulls. "In the future let our people live together in peace."

"It is good," Hump replied through Rebecca's interpretation.

Quietly as they had come, the soldiers departed. When the last of them crested the rise, Lone Wolf came to where Rebecca stood, watching, outside the lodge where Grover Ridgeway rested. He put a friendly hand on her shoulder.

"So much for a pleasant return home," she said bitterly.

"It wasn't our doing," Lone Wolf suggested.

"True. But somehow it all seems so futile. One day, before very long, Hump and all the Śayaota will have to move onto the reservation or be exterminated. Bryce Peyton wasn't alone in his sentiments, nor was Alystaire Carmoody. It . . . makes me so sad."

"What next?"

"I don't know. I'm not sure of what I want or where I want to go. But it will have to be somewhere far from here. Someplace peaceful."

"No." Grover Ridgeway spoke firmly from the entrance to the tipi. He swayed slightly and his skin was pale, but he had complete command of his voice. "You're not going anywhere far from here at all. You're coming back to the Slash-R-Bar as my wife."

All the bitterness and anguish Rebecca had compressed into her bosom melted in a rush and a marvelous giddiness swept over her. He meant it. He really meant it! On unsteady legs she stepped to Grover's side.

"Yes, oh yes, Grover. If that's what you want. I—I think . . . I'm going to cry!"

"No, you don't," her future husband commanded. "Not my sweet girl."

"If—if you say so, Grover. And I'll always, always be."

"What?"

"Your sweet girl."

221

SHELTER
by Paul Ledd